No Other Choice

No Other Choice

Lissa Halls Johnson

Power Books

Fleming H. Revell Company
Old Tappan, New Jersey

Library of Congress Cataloging-in-Publication Data

Johnson, Lissa Halls.
    No other choice.

    I. Title.
PS3560.037975N6   1986   813'.54   86-622
ISBN 0-8007-5221-X

For MFA . . .
May God heal all your wounds.
Thank you
for sharing your life with me.

Oh my Baby Child.
I never knew
I would love you so much.
I thought I was doing the best for all of us.
Now you are gone.
Oh my Baby Child.
To have a minute of time,
to hold you and kiss you.
But then I could never let you go.
I see you,
My little one,
In every place I look.
I see your braids chase you
as you ride your bike.
I hear your shrieks of laughter,
from the playground nearby.
I see your freckled nose,
in the middle of a peanut butter and jelly face.
I see your baseball cap,
that's too big for your tousled brown hair.
I rock you each night in my dreams,
singing lullabies through tears.
Oh my Baby Child.
I never knew.
I just never knew.
And now my heart breaks,
My Baby Child.

·1·

"**T**his is it, babe," David said as he laced his fingers through Joann's. "Scared?"

"No! Excited's more like it." *I'm starting over,* Joann thought with a smile. *The slate is wiped clean. What's past is past.* She climbed into the U-Haul truck, scooting next to David. "You look like a truck driver," she told him.

He laughed. "It's the muscles, my dear," he said in his Arnold Schwarzenegger imitation.

The truck pulled out of the driveway from the apartment where she and David spent their first wonderful year of marriage. Lighthearted, Joann waved good-bye. By leaving Los Angeles, she left the nightmares, the blackness, and the memories that had clouded her marriage. *The new start will help me be cheerful again, like I was in high school.* Memories of laughter spilled in, prompting pictures of happiness in her head—she and her best friend, Carolyn, playing practical jokes on each other, always with hours of laughing no matter what they did. In the graduation edition of her school newspaper, someone had stated, "Joann Miller leaves, the most contented and happy person we know."

She believed them, confidently enrolling in college, looking forward to continuing her happiness and education. Years of confusion followed instead, where every turn seemed both right and wrong. Ugly and desperate decisions were made. She had vowed never to tell David about Ross and what they had done. Those memories didn't belong in her new life.

The baby she carried now, a tiny thing inside of her, would wipe away the last of the ugliness, memories she would never have to face now that she was leaving it all behind.

David squeezed her hand, then let go to hold the steering wheel. The scenery flew past the truck windows, the tires emitting a loud hum, the cab constantly bouncing. Apartments lined the freeway, then houses, then houses spaced far apart with chickens in the yards.

The truck droned over hills, past Magic Mountain Amusement Park to the Grapevine Highway through the mountains. On the other side of the Grapevine, the great San Joaquin valley stretched out before them.

"I hope you don't feel pushed into this move," Joann said. She leaned her head against his shoulder, not wanting to look at him while she talked. "Since Carolyn and I have been friends for so long, and you don't know Rob very well, I was afraid. . . ."

"Pushed? Are you kidding? It's terrific!" David kissed her on the head. "Look, babe. Rob and I got to be quick friends that time we went on the retreat before we were married. Besides, I love Lake Ridge. I've wanted to get away from Los Angeles for more years than you have. So why not Lake Ridge?"

Why not Lake Ridge indeed? The farther away from Los Angeles the better. It eliminated the possibility of chance meetings with Ross. Once had been horrible and uncomfortable enough. Now he was the head of "his" beloved psychology department, married, and the father of the son he always wanted. Lake Ridge. No more reminders of the decision she had had to make.

She shook her head. She promised herself not to think about Ross anymore. She would no longer be haunted by the desire to see him alone . . . even to talk, or share the past over dinner, or have one more hug. . . .

How ridiculous to even want those things, she thought, glancing at

David, hoping he couldn't detect the betrayal of her thoughts. *And why am I fleeing the chance meetings, and wishing for planned ones? It's good I'm getting out before it's too late.*

David tapped the gearshift knob. "This is certainly a strange way to celebrate an anniversary. You don't mind, do you?"

"I don't mind, David. I'm just so glad to be getting out of L.A." She did mind, a little. Her dreams always seemed to get crushed—even the one about the perfect anniversary. She planned to have a nice candlelight dinner somewhere, not bouncing in a rental truck, towing a dented blue Datsun behind. But what made her think her anniversary would be any different from the wedding?

* * *

She and Carolyn had drawn up wedding plans in high school one night, armed with three issues of *Bride's* magazine. Joann had sketched pictures of her attendants wearing wide-brimmed hats, trimmed with roses and baby's breath. Her gown would be a pristine white satin, trimmed with a thousand pearls. The day would be a misty haze of joy and love, to treasure always.

She and David married on the first of May—a day of abundant colors, flowers, and beauty.

She had gotten her dream dress, and the attendants had their hats with baby's breath, but no roses. The day was filled with rushing around, last-minute disasters of ripped hems and fluttery stomachs instead of the anticipated misty joy. The late-arriving photographer rushed through the picture taking. It all seemed unreal.

The veil over her face masked her confusion and fear that perhaps she wasn't doing the right thing in marrying David. Her shoulder-length brown hair didn't curl the way she wanted. She liked fluffy, wispy curls. She got tight ringlets that insisted on clinging together. She decided it didn't look too bad when she saw the picture where the photographer managed to catch the glint of red in her hair as the morning sun came through the church window.

David, standing tall among his groomsmen, wore a deep brown tux with short tails. The tailor had fitted him so you couldn't see the strength of his body. Each step she took, she saw one more detail she loved. His golden brown mustache, always neatly trimmed; his hair a shade darker than the mustache. When she got right up to him and looked into his dark blue eyes, her eyes filled with tears, and for a moment, she imagined she saw Ross standing before her instead of David. She hated herself for that.

David later told her that the smile she gave him made him feel no one else was in the room.

* * *

No, she thought, *my dreams aren't really crushed, just twisted into a parody.*

She shifted positions in the uncomfortable truck. "How long is it going to take to get there?"

David chewed on his bottom lip. "From Los Angeles to Lake Ridge is five hundred sixty-three miles, it takes ten hours by car, and maybe a couple more by truck. We should be there about seven, I guess."

Joann put her foot up on the dashboard. "Seven more hours in this thing?"

" 'Fraid so." David took a deep breath. "Just think. No more smog. I think I've forgotten what blue sky looks like."

Yes, Joann thought, *this is a time to forget ugly things and experience new, beautiful things. Things like building my relationship with David.* Sweet, persistent David, who had done his best to capture her attention that day on the beach.

Her friend Carolyn had urged her to go on the beach outing with the new church she attended. Joann didn't want to go, her experiences making her feel so much older than they. Desperate and lonely, she agreed to go, hoping that because of her small size, she would easily get lost in the crowd.

The minute Joann reclined on her towel, she wished she hadn't come. Carolyn laid her towel next to Joann's, then left, never to return until the end of the day. Joann watched as she flitted about, the beautiful butterfly visiting every flower, male or female, feeling lonelier with each person Carolyn spent time with.

Several of the young men came to talk to Joann, trying their best to win her attention. One even told her that her brown eyes, large and innocent, drew him to her. She smiled, polite but not talkative. She didn't respond to them, so they didn't stay long.

The grinding truck gears broke into her memories. "What's going on in there?" David asked, tapping her on the head.

She looked at him and smiled. "I'm remembering how we met."

David tipped his head back and laughed. "With all those sharks after you, I felt someone with a little class had to come to your rescue."

"I needed rescuing?"

"Sure you did. Especially from George. I hated to see such a nice girl like you caught in the clutches of that creep."

12

"Well, thanks. I remember that you were the only one persistent enough to come back three times to attempt a conversation. I was awfully rude."

"I didn't think you were rude. I thought you were lonely. Lonely people are afraid to talk."

"Who told you that?"

"I figured it out myself."

"Well, you *were* persistent."

"I'm glad I was, too."

"Me too."

David had done more than be persistent that day. He didn't try to intrude. He brought over his own towel and sat next to her, instead of sitting on her towel as the others had. He didn't try to talk about her past, only the present and the future. When Joann finally decided to talk to him, they didn't lack for conversation. They became fast friends, not realizing until two years had passed that they were in love.

How different the love she had had for Ross and her love for David. With David, her love was subdued, cautious, incomplete, yet comfortable, contrasted with the wild and myopic love she shared with Ross. *Calm* best described her love for David. She knew David loved her more than she could ever love him. She could never allow herself to be as vulnerable to another man again. She would always hold something back.

David accepted her. On the night he asked her to marry him—at the same beach two years later—she hesitated to say yes. "You might not want me if you knew what I've done," she told him. He assured her that the past would not be used against her. After all, his life hadn't been perfect either. He confessed to childhood stealing and some rowdiness in high school at the drinking parties everyone took turns hosting.

Joann almost laughed at the pettiness of what he had done, compared to her own sins. But now she left them all behind—the pain, the tears, the anger, the betrayal.

Joann fiddled with the radio knob again, trying to receive a better signal than a two-station blend of static. David reached over and turned it off. "Forget the dumb thing. Let's talk."

"Okay, so talk," she said.

David's brows pulled together. "I wish you wouldn't do that. It makes me feel stupid, and I can't say anything."

"Sorry. I was just teasing."

"I know. . . ."

Trying to lighten up the mood, Joann made a big exhibition of looking out the window. "David, look at all the cows! Thousands of them! Miles of them!"

"Pew! And mountains of their leftovers, from the smell of things."

"Can you imagine living out here?"

"A real cow town."

They both laughed. *It's good being with David*, Joann thought. *He's so easygoing.* "This is really out in the middle of nowhere."

"And Lake Ridge isn't?"

Joann shrugged. "It seems to have everything it needs."

"People, water, toilets, *telephones*."

Joann slapped his arm. "Grocery stores, a theater, a hospital. . . ."

"And streets that roll up at eight o'clock."

"Okay, okay, so the town is a little on the slow side."

"A little? Don't you remember the movie Carolyn said just came to the theater? We saw that a year ago, and it wasn't all that new then."

"As usual, you win." Joann gave him a light kiss on his unshaven cheek.

"I like to win. I always get a nice lady to give me the victory-circle kiss."

By the time they passed through Sacramento, excitement melted into fatigue. The endless bouncing and noisy tires pressed Joann's head into an ache. Turning off the highway, David forced the truck around curves and over hills. Joann watched the craggy hills covered with rocks and oak trees which reached their arthritic fingers out, unable to grasp what they reached for.

For many miles, the road followed a rugged creek sandwiched between the road and the rocky hillside. David had to pull over three times for a nauseated Joann, and five times for cars that stacked up behind him. A school of puffy clouds swam past in the ocean of sky, the remnants of a spring storm. Then finally, they caught a glimpse of the lake, and Joann emitted a feeble hooray.

The truck rumbled down Main Street, taking up every inch available. Joann noticed every clothing and specialty store they passed, while David noticed the western motif facades on nearly every building. Everything but the bars and one restaurant was closed. "Streets are rolled up early, I see," David announced.

Joann poked him in the ribs. "Don't make fun."

David's mustache twitched. "How can I *not* make fun of this town?"

Main Street took a sharp left by the pizza parlor, then wound to the right, passing the grocery store where David would begin work in one week. The road curved to the right again, heading straight for the lake.

"Oh, David," Joann exclaimed. "The lake is as beautiful as I remembered it."

David pointed at the dormant volcano. "Mount Sakar. I don't think I'll ever get tired of looking at that."

"Or the lake. . . ."

"Or the lake."

They followed the lakeshore road about a mile, only looking away from the lake as they passed the apartment they would move into the next day. They drove on another mile, then turned up a dirt road. It led past a broken-down mobile home, up a hill to a small, new home at the top of a rise. The spring mud stuck to the bottom of their shoes as they walked across the driveway to the path that led to the house. David had one foot on the path when the door flew open and two people rushed out of the house.

·2·

·A·t 7:30 that morning, Carolyn shifted her weight from one slender foot to the other, reaching down to touch her toe. Right, left, right, left. As the music picked up the pace, Carolyn switched to jumping jacks as a warm-up for her jog around the room. Each movement, precise and vigorous, produced sweat beads that slid into her lavender headband. Earlier, she had lifted small dumbbells, increasing the strength in her arms. As the song ended, she fastened ankle weights in place before beginning her jog.

Carolyn ran an extra five minutes to make up for the doughnut she planned to have with breakfast. She ignored the phone that rang ten times before it quit.

She saved her favorite music for the cool-down. Always mellow, sometimes jazz, sometimes Bach, sometimes Renaissance flute or guitar. Her mind relaxed with her, forgetting for the moment her concerns and projects.

No one understood her need to exercise every day, no matter what. Even sickness didn't deter her much. She might cut the routine a bit, and move slower, but she never missed a day.

But then, few people understood her fervor about anything. Each summer of Carloyn's high-school years, she left her baffled parents to spend two months at Mexican orphanages where she cooked, washed clothes, and played with dirty children. The children loved her, the administrators favored her. She was dependable, able, and willing to do anything asked of her. If she hated a job, she never showed it. She seemed to know what to do to brighten someone's day.

Even now, Carolyn tried to get to her favorite orphanage for at least one week a year. Her husband, Rob, went too, to help straighten out the finances if there were any problems.

Her cool-down complete, Carolyn grabbed her Bible for a few minutes of meditation and prayer before hopping into the shower. There was so much work to do this day that each minute was calculated and labeled.

Her wet hair swirled about her head in natural blonde curls. With swift, automatic motions, she pushed at them in handfuls, encouraging them to curl more. She cracked an egg in the pan, and turned to open the cupboard behind her, pulling a plate from the stack. She touched the pictures taped to the door, one of a five-year-old boy, and the other of a seven-year-old girl, saying a prayer for each of them. These kids were "hers." She paid support for them to go to school, sent them gifts, and even went to visit them in their ghetto home in Los Angeles.

She scolded herself as she put the old-fashioned doughnut on her plate next to the egg, then smiled at herself. *Everyone can have a vice or two*, she thought.

She had always loved to give of herself, and of her time. Her fire and enthusiasm swept up everyone even remotely in her path.

In the back of her mind hung a motto in flashing neon lights. "If there is anything worth doing, it's worth doing with a passion."

She swigged the last of her milk, dabbed her finger in her plate to pick up the last doughnut crumbs. She folded the newspaper, regretting that she would not be able to read it today. Her old friend Joann, and husband, David, were to arrive in a U-Haul, ready to plant themselves in this little town.

Her regular work would have to be juggled with the extra work needed to get ready for her guests. She wished Rob could be of more help, but he would not get home from the office until just about the time Joann and David were scheduled to arrive.

The truck pulled in at 7:45, almost an hour later than anticipated. Two weary people dropped to the ground from the cab. Carolyn and Rob gave each a hug, then led them inside. "It's so good to see you," Carolyn said.

"And even better to see you," replied Joann.

"We would have been here on time," David said, "if Joann didn't ask to stop at every gas station along the way."

Joann's face flushed. "David, I can't help it."

David smiled. "It's the end of the day, and Joann can't take a joke."

Joann cocked her head and gave him a weary look, which wasn't hard.

"Take off your shoes here," Carolyn said, pointing next to the front door. "If you leave them upside down, the mud should be dried by tomorrow, and we can clean them easier."

"Carolyn, I can't get over your house," Joann exclaimed. "Every time I see it, I think I'm stepping into a magazine."

Carolyn's pride showed on her face. She loved to have people compliment her on her home. She had chosen each piece of furniture with care, matching and blending the colors of the pictures, wallpapers, and drapes to make each room more than pleasant to be in.

She stuffed a towel and washcloth into Joann's hands. "Since you are most eager to use the bathroom, you may also be the first to take a shower."

"Thanks."

Joann emerged fifteen minutes later, looking refreshed. Carolyn shoved David in the direction of the bathroom, also with towel and cloth. "Your turn, smelly."

"Hey, watch who you're talking to."

Carolyn ignored him, turning to face Joann. "You look almost human. Sit down, I've made you dinner." She pointed to a TV tray, on which sat a pastrami on rye sandwich.

"Thanks and thanks," Joann replied sarcastically and gratefully. "I didn't need such extravagance," she said, indicating the ruffled place mat with matching napkin rolled neatly inside a ceramic bird napkin ring. A crystal goblet of juice sat in the corner of the tray. In the other corner, a small bud vase held a miniature rosebud.

"That's not extravagant," Carolyn replied sincerely.

Joann caught sight of unflappable Rob, trying not to laugh. "What's so funny?"

Caught, Rob sat up and adjusted his tortoiseshell glasses. "Funny? Nothing's funny."

"Rob, when you are hunched over, shoulders twitching, with your finger under your nose, you are laughing. Granted, no one else in this world laughs that way, but for you, it is a laugh."

Rob looked at Carolyn. "I hate friends who know you well." He turned to Joann. "Really, it's not important."

"Well now that we've made such a big deal out of it," Joann said, "I'm dying to know what you thought was funny. Especially since you never laugh at the truly funny. Only the twisted, demented sort of funny."

He looked at her like a startled squirrel. "Okay. If you promise not to get mad at him."

"Him? Him who?"

"Him in the shower."

Joann turned to Carolyn. "Accountants can add, but not talk, I see."

"You started it."

"Started what?"

"Never mind."

"Okay, Rob, what did David say?"

"David just said," Rob's hunched shoulders began to twitch, and his finger went under his nose, "that eating here is like eating at Ma Maison while eating at home is like having a Tommy Burger every night. Greasy, sloppy, and served on wax paper."

With that, Rob could contain himself no longer. He actually let out a real and true guffaw, to Carolyn's amazement.

Joann slammed her sandwich down on the plate. "Oooh, I'll kill him!" She picked up the tray, putting it down so hard, some of the juice sloshed on the place mat. Carolyn jumped to get a cloth.

Rob called, "Joann, you promised!"

Joann marched to the bathroom and flung open the door. "A Tommy Burger? A *Tommy Burger?*"

David's voice came through the rush of water. "You traitor, Rob!"

As Carolyn finished mopping up the spill, replacing the soggy place mat with a clean one, Joann marched back to her seat, stuffing a handful of clothes under her chair, replaced the tray, and resumed eating.

Carolyn put on her tolerant look, but inside, she loved every minute of it. She had taught Joann all she knew about being vindictive and how to take the perfect revenge. She savored the moment before speaking. "Joann, I've finally found my calling."

"Yeah, Carolyn? What is it this time? Nukes? Cute little baby seals?"

"Nope. But I'll tell you later. I want you guys to settle in first."

"You won't forget to tell me, will you?" she asked between bites.

"Of course not. I expect you to help me out."

Joann nodded, drinking the last of her juice. "Sure, if I can."

Screams came from the bathroom. "Where are my clothes, Joanna?"

Carolyn smiled. "He must be mad if he's calling you Joanna."

Joann returned the smile, smug and mischievous.

Carolyn thought the door would come off the hinges. A waist-wrapped, dripping figure appeared, water from his hair creating little rivulets down his face and dropping off his chin and the end of his nose.

"David, you mustn't get Carolyn's carpet wet," Joann said as if nothing had happened. "You know how careful she is."

"Go ahead and say it, Joann," Carolyn said. She turned to David. "How picky I am, David."

"I don't believe it, Rob is laughing again," Joann said.

Rob's finger pressed tight against his upper lip, causing a bloodless white halo to surround his finger. His shoulders twitched faster than Carolyn had ever seen.

"I want my clothes!" David sputtered, water dripping from his mustache.

The demand hung in the air for precisely three seconds, then shattered into laughter around him.

"Come and get them if you're so desperate," Joann teased.

David, full of indignity, tiptoed over. One hand clutched his towel in strategic position around his waist, the other reached for the clothes. Joann grabbed the outstretched hand, and pulled him close for a kiss. She tugged playfully at the towel. "If it wasn't for Carolyn, I'd do it."

"Well, in that case, I'll do it for you." David whipped off the towel to a duet of shrieks.

"Where did you get those?" Joann demanded.

"You don't think I'd take a shower and put on dirty shorts do you? I hung them on the back of the door. . . ."

"Get out of here," Joann said, stuffing the clothes in his arms, and slapping his behind.

Carolyn wondered if Rob's finger ached. It looked like he wasn't quite certain whether to wipe the tears from underneath his glasses, or to maintain his finger hold. She shook her head. "The only person in the world I have seen make Rob laugh is David. Then I worry whether he will burst something in the process."

Carolyn whisked away Joann's plate the moment the last bite of sandwich disappeared. In a moment she was back again, carrying a rosette-laden cake with a single candle blazing from the middle. "Happy Anniversary, Happy Anniversary . . ." she and Rob sang.

Joann's hands dropped in her lap, the corners of her mouth turned down at the edges. Carolyn knew that look which came whenever Joann felt surprised and overwhelmed. David, on the other hand, always knew what to say. "Hey! All right! It'd better be chocolate."

"David! How rude!" Joann said.

"Don't get huffy, Jo. I just want to know whether I want a gigantic piece, or whether I'll have to settle for huge. No harm in that, is there?"

Joann rolled her eyes at Carolyn. "There's no getting culture into this one."

Carolyn answered David. "Of course, it's chocolate. I do have a memory, you know."

David and Joann looked at her, confusion on both faces.

"Your wedding cake was chocolate. Or has it been so long that you've forgotten?"

Joann scrunched up her nose like a bunny. "Of course I remembered, but I didn't think anyone else would."

"How could I forget, Joann? Not too many people buck tradition for chocolate cake. Besides, David is an avid chocoholic. One does not forget having a full box of See's candies disappear in one night."

"Hey, how did you know it was me?" David protested.

"You were the only one who had the look of the cat that ate the canary. The real giveaway came when you denied having anything to do with it, chocolate hiding in the corners of your mouth."

"Okay, okay, so I ate your chocolates. Now give me a gigantic piece of that cake with a tall glass of milk."

"David!"

"Sorry."

The men won Trivial Pursuit. Carolyn hated to lose. "We would have won if we didn't get two dumb questions about boxing."

David shrugged his shoulders with pride. "That's what you get for not being a well-rounded human being." He glanced at Rob. "No pun intended."

Too late for apologies, Rob's shoulders were shaking again.

Carolyn shook her head. "I don't know what to do with your husband, Joann. He's a nuisance."

"Don't I know it," Joann said. "But I'm stuck with him now."

David leaned back on the couch, his hands behind his head. He closed his eyes. "Yep, some people get all the luck."

Carolyn packed the game away, careful to replace each item as she had found it the first time she opened the box. She turned to her guests. "The second room to your left is ready for you. I hope you'll find the bed comfortable. Good night."

With that, she shooed them to their room, turned off the lights, and joined Rob, who had managed to shed his clothes and fall asleep before she got there.

·3·

·· Joann looked at David. "Can you believe this?" Their bed was turned down, with a small mint on each pillow. She would have laughed, if she hadn't known Carolyn so well, and knew that this was not done as a joke.

David snatched a mint. "Can I have yours too?"

"No!"

Joann crawled into the bed, thankful for her new life to be shared with old friends. A minute later she was asleep.

* * *

From the warmth came a noise. She held her hands over her ears, trying in vain to shut it out. She tried to snuggle deeper into the soft bed. The noise grew louder and louder, and she thought her eardrums would burst. She began to moan, curling up against the noise. Louder. Blacker and blacker the air grew around her. Thick. She thought she would suffocate. The noise came up around her throat, pulling tighter. Tighter.

Joann's eyes popped open. She stared into the night, shaking, sweating. Terrified. Afraid to close her eyes again. Afraid of that awful noise, the strangulating blackness. Her lungs felt as if she had been running. Her hair was drenched. Sweat in the middle of a cold night. She turned to stare at the digital clock. As several numbers flickered past, she felt safe enough to slip into the bathroom to change her nightclothes. Since all her other nightgowns were packed in the truck, she opened David's satchel and pulled out a white undershirt. She pulled it over her head and slipped back under the covers.

David rolled over. "What is it, Jo?" he muttered, throwing his arm over her. He fumbled around a moment with the shirt. "Another one?"

Joann nodded as a little affirming squeak managed its way out.

"Sorry." David patted her arm and in less than a minute had resumed his soft snore.

Joann, exhausted and afraid to fall asleep, began to pray. "God, I deserve this, don't I? But I'm scared. Do You still love me? Will You hold my babies again for me? God, You know I had to do it. Being pregnant would have ruined everyone—Ross, my parents, me." Tears rolled down her cheeks, adding wetness to the already damp pillow. All energy to stay awake gone, she fell back asleep.

Joann woke to the sound of the shower running. Sounds of breathing came from somewhere underneath the pillow next to her. She reached over, gently stroking David's arm. It moved, lifting the pillow a few inches. A squinting sleepy eye looked at her. A second later, a sleepy smile joined the squint. The pillow dropped down, and the arm reached over to pull her close. "David," she whispered. "David." She lifted the pillow off his ear. "Please don't tell Carolyn."

"Tell her what?" David looked confused. He looked at the T-shirt, then seemed to remember. "Why, babe?"

"I don't know. I guess because I feel stupid about them."

"Okay," he said in a sigh. "I just wish you'd find somebody to talk to about them. It makes me feel so helpless to see you so terrified by a dream."

"I know. I'll get over them."

David frowned. "You've had them ever since we've been married, and who knows how long before that. You certainly won't tell me."

She bit her lip for a moment. "Just don't tell Carolyn, okay?"

"Yeah, right." Perturbed, David turned over, pulling the pillow, like a wall between them, back over his head.

* * *

The sweat dripped down the faces of the two men, one used to lifting crates of fruits and vegetables, the other used to lifting a pen, ledger books, and floppy disks. "Ever hear of the Bible verse about being unequally yoked?" David asked.

Rob nodded.

"It sure applies now."

Rob's shoulders began to twitch as Carolyn flew by with a box in her arms.

"Sorry, guys," Joann said. "I feel so stupid just sitting around."

"Yeah, sure," Carolyn replied. "I'll just bet you're pregnant. You don't look it. You don't even get sick in the morning."

"Isn't it wonderful? I didn't know I was pregnant for a while because I wasn't getting sick." *I thought you got sick every time you got pregnant.*

"A first timer's luck, I guess," said Carolyn, wiping off her forehead with a raggy tissue.

"Sure," Joann replied quietly. She tried to get the subject back to its original track. "I really am sorry I can't help. I don't want to take any chances on losing this baby."

"Is everyone this concerned about losing a baby when they get pregnant?"

Joann felt a quiver run through her stomach. "Probably not. I suppose I'm more paranoid than most since I lost one already."

"I forgot about that. Oh, Joann, I'm sorry. I was surprised you got pregnant so soon after you got married. I didn't think you had planned on starting your family immediately."

"Are you kidding? We did plan it. We wanted to have a baby right away."

Carolyn looked skeptical, but kept quiet. "Well, go ahead and take it easy. You can do the same for me when I get pregnant. I'll carry the whip, you can be the slave. . . ." Carolyn was out the door to fetch another box before she finished her sentence.

Joann patted the tiny mound of growing baby. "You'll like it here," she whispered. "A brand-new apartment, the lake right across the street. We can't get to it since houses are built right along the shore. But we can see it. And we can go to the beach at the park. . . ."

"Who're you talking to?" Carolyn looked baffled. She set her box down on the dusty kitchen counter.

Joann thought her face must have rivaled Santa's suit. "The baby."

A quizzical look crossed Carolyn's face, *as though I must be the strangest person who ever walked the earth,* Joann thought. The look reminded Joann of the nurse who had taken care of her when she had her miscarriage.

* * *

The nurse couldn't understand Joann's anger, or her sorrow. "You'll be able to have another one. It ain't the end of the world. Happens to lots of women. You'll get over it."

The nurse was a nightmare. The whole thing was a nightmare. It had begun with a nightmare.

She felt pulled, drenched in pain that came in waves, crashing over her until she struggled, and woke. But the pain still pressed on her, the bed wet, not with sweat, but with blood of her baby's life.

She cried all the way to the hospital, knowing the child she longed for was not to be. She didn't feel sorry for David then. When he reached his loving hand over to touch hers, she slapped it away, curling up as close to the car door as she could, stuffing another towel underneath her.

The hospital staff, neither cold nor caring, took her in, did their job, and sent her home. The one nurse jabbed her with a needle and then her words. Others, more kind, patted her on the arm, unable to comfort her with their words. It wasn't enough. Nothing would ever be enough.

The next day, she stayed in bed. David brought her some chicken soup and a new novel she had been wanting to read. She stayed curled up in a little ball, never saying thanks.

David came back later to take away the cold soup and to brush the hair away from her face. She didn't want him to be nice. She didn't deserve it anyway.

"Babe, I'm sorry," David said.

Joann turned away from his voice. "No, you're not."

She heard him sigh in frustration. "It was my baby, too," he said after a minute's silence.

Joann's tears began to soak the pillow, and then turned into sobs. She didn't reject his arms that wrapped around her, and their tears mingled together.

"God took our baby away."

"He'll give us another one."

"I wish I could believe that." *I took one away from God, now He took one away from me. Are we even now? Or is my body permanently damaged?*

* * *

Carolyn trudged in, struggling with an oversized box. She dropped it in the middle of the kitchen floor. "I don't know about you, lazy, but the rest of us are hungry. I'm going to Foster Freeze to get us a hamburger."

"Great. I'm sorry I didn't think about it."

"That's okay. It'll be a good excuse for me to quit for a while anyway."

Joann opened a box and began to unload, newsprint turning her fingers black.

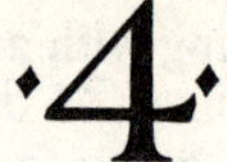

·· A week of scrubbing hadn't removed all the newprint from Joann's fingers. They looked as though she'd been rebuilding a car engine. She hung up the smudged phone; Carolyn was coming over to help her hang pictures.

Carolyn had a gift for decorating that Joann envied, and the money to carry it through. Joann liked her home to look neat and attractive, but she didn't have much to work with—neither the proper furniture nor money. She looked around at the hodgepodge of cast-off furniture that decorated the living room: watermelon crates for end tables, a TV with three popsicle sticks wedged in the tuner, and two sofas with violently clashing patterns. She knew the hodgepodge look would disappear when Carolyn worked her magic, using Joann's handcrafts to hang on the walls. But Joann still couldn't stop the little pangs of jealousy over the difference in their homes and furniture.

Joann shouldn't have been surprised that Carolyn didn't comment about her furniture. Carolyn had seen it unloaded from the truck and didn't comment then either. But Joann still had fears that Carolyn would throw up her hands and declare the apartment a disaster before she even started. Instead, Carolyn marched in, deciding to begin with the hallway.

"By the way, Carolyn, you never did get a chance to tell me about your new crusade the other night. What is it this time?" Joann asked as she pulled framed photographs from the carton.

Carolyn adjusted a family portrait on the wall before she answered. "Abortion," she said, smiling.

Joann's heart stopped. "Abortion?"

The smile left as she turned to Joann. "Yeah. Abortion."

Joann wanted to say something clever, but she stared instead.

Carolyn's eyes saddened. She turned away to choose another photograph from the stack on the floor. "It hurts me to see all these babies swept away like they are nothing."

Joann felt her breathing get rougher, and the tears come to her eyes.

Carolyn didn't seem to find what she wanted. She sat on the floor and picked up a nail from the box. "It's got to be stopped, Joann, before there are no children left."

Joann hated crying in front of people. She turned her head as Carolyn reached for her hand. "Oh, I'm sorry, Joann. I forget you lost one, too. The subject of abortion must hurt you terribly, too. After all, you lost one you wanted, while those other women just wipe out what is inconvenient."

Joann began to sob. She hurried to the bathroom to get a tissue.

Carolyn followed her. "Look, I'm sorry. Maybe we can talk about it some other time. I think you'd be a great asset to our group."

Joann nodded, agreeing with the not talking, but not to joining the group.

Carolyn put a comforting arm around her shoulder. "Why is it so tough for some people to lose a child, and for others. . . ."

A sob stuck in Joann's chest, making her cough.

Carolyn gave her shoulder another squeeze. "I'll go finish hanging the pictures."

Joann nodded her approval, and sat down in the bathroom to finish her cry.

She ran cool water over a washcloth and held it up to her face, cooling the fire beneath the skin, behind her eyes. She pulled the cloth away, inspecting the damage to her makeup in the mirror.

Oh God, You don't give up, do You? You will punish me for the rest of my life for this. You hate me as much as I hate myself, I suppose. She hung the wrung-out cloth in the shower, emerging as a subdued and controlled woman. "Sorry I fell apart, Carolyn. That subject does weird things to me."

"It does weird things to lots of people. Nothing weirder than those who choose it, though." Her head shook in disbelief.

Joann clenched her teeth, counting silently to five. Choosing a photo of her family in earlier years, she held it up to Carolyn for approval. "How about putting this one here?"

"I think so. Here. Let's try it."

Feeling stronger, Joann asked what she hoped would be a safer question. "What made you choose abortion for your newest bandwagon?"

Carolyn took the nail out of her mouth, scratched the entry point on the wall, then gestured for the hammer. "I suppose Billy had a lot to do with it, and Susanna. They are such important people in my life, and I can't imagine my life without them."

"Susanna? Your cousin?"

"Did you know she's adopted?"

"No, I didn't. She looks so much like your family."

"Can you believe it? I'm certain God had her chosen for our family from the very beginning. Anyway, she's so special. I hate the thought of her not being here, of her mother not caring enough to give her life."

Joann searched for another photo, trying to keep her emotions under control. "How old is Billy? I always forget."

"He's ten."

"How is he these days?"

"He's just the same. Every year we can look back and say he's matured just a little bit more. The doctors say he'll never be more than three years old in mental age, but he does learn some little things that a three-year-old wouldn't learn."

With the last picture hung in the hallway, they both walked toward the master bedroom as if on cue. "I don't know what my life would be like without Billy, either," Carolyn said. "I was such a selfish jerk before he was born. He has taught me compassion, patience, and a love for things and people not quite perfect."

"Isn't life difficult for your parents?" Joann asked as she pulled her huge teddy bear from inside a box. Poor thing had been stuffed in as protection for the pictures. Carolyn sat on the bed, outlining the quilt with her fingernails. It seemed hard for her to answer. "It is very difficult for my parents. I know they wish Billy was normal. Any parent would. So I asked them that same question once."

"And?"

"Dad reached for Mom's hand, squeezing it. Then they both looked at Billy. Each one spoke just a few words at a time, saying, 'Suffering and joy are sometimes closely intertwined. Without one, it seems, you can't have the other. Billy has caused us tremendous amounts of suffering we've many times wished we could do without. But at the same time, he has brought us such joy we never would have known if he wasn't a part of our lives. If we had been given the choice, to have Billy or not, we couldn't make it. We're glad God made the choice for us.' "

Joann sat holding her bear in her arms, stroking it like a child.

Carolyn's fingernails followed the patterns on the quilt, hovering momentarily over a quilted bird. "If I were a bird," she whispered.

The stroking stopped, and Joann looked at Carolyn.

Carolyn shook her head and waved her hand in the air. "Just something Billy always says."

Together they unwrapped the mementos and wall hangings for the room. "Joann, you never cease to amaze me," Carolyn remarked as she lifted a wall hanging from the tissue.

Feeling embarrassed and proud, Joann tried but failed to keep the smile from her face. "What do you mean?"

"You and that sewing machine, thread and thimble, create some of the most beautiful things I've ever seen."

"You think so?"

"Oh, come on, Miss Humble Pie. This is gorgeous!"

Surprised, Joann replied, "Big deal. I took a lace panel from a store, and threw it together with scraps of fabric."

"I don't know. There's more to it than that. The ruffle, the contrasting lace, peach ribbon to match the delicate peach fabric. Only the eye of an artist can put these kinds of things together."

"Who're you calling an artist? I can't draw a stick figure worth looking at," Joann laughed.

"Who needs to draw to be an artist? Certainly not you."

"Not you either. You are an artist in the way you can decorate, and make junk look good."

"What is this, the mutual admiration society?"

Joann laughed. "What else are friends for? If we don't pat each other on the back, then who will?"

"Good point. Anyway, put one of these on my Christmas list if you think you're going to give me something this year."

"Since when did I give you Christmas presents?"

"Since we met in high school."

"Hah! You call that record single of 'Merry Christmas, Darling' a present?"

"Do you call getting a hand-knit scarf a present?"

"I worked for hours on that thing," Joann countered.

"But who needs a snow scarf in Los Angeles?"

"Who needs incense?"

"It was cheap," Carolyn said.

"I'll make you a deal. Since our Christmas presents always bombed, I'll forget Christmas this year if you will, and I'll make a baby quilt if you ever decide to get pregnant."

Carolyn's face blanched, her hand holding the hammer dropped to her side. "Joann, don't you know?"

"Guess not. Are you already pregnant?"

"No. And I may never be. Rob and I have been trying for three years."

"Why didn't you tell me?"

"I'm sorry. I shouldn't act like you ought to know. We've never told anyone. It's such a private thing, you know?"

"Then why'd you joke about getting pregnant on moving day?"

Carolyn looked thoughtful. "I can talk about it on my own terms, make my own jokes. But sometimes when I get caught off guard, I'm surprised at how much it hurts."

"Well, you're only twenty-six. You've got lots of years to try."

"Yeah, I guess so," Carolyn replied, not sounding convinced. She pounded the nail into the wall, then whirled around, anger filling her face. "If only one of those selfish women would think about someone else for a change, maybe I could have that baby."

"Excuse me," Joann said in her calmest voice, forcing herself to walk at a normal pace from the room. She ducked into the bathroom, fighting tears again. Carolyn made her feel so guilty. It wasn't fair! She didn't know what it was like to be nineteen and pregnant and scared and confused. Joann felt responsible for Carolyn not having a child. *It's people like me*, she thought, *who have snatched the baby right out of her arms.*

Don't take the load of the world's problems on yourself, a little voice inside said. *You had no other choice. You did what was best.*

Joann flushed the toilet for effect, then rejoined Carolyn. They hung pictures in silence for a long time.

"Want some lunch?"

"Sure, as long as you don't serve grilled peanut butter sandwiches again."

"What's wrong with them? They're terrific."

Carolyn rolled her eyes. "Tuna is more to my liking."

"You'll have to make it yourself then. Now that I'm pregnant, it makes me gag."

Bread and knives were pulled from the drawers, the cast iron skillet put on the stove to heat. Joann dropped the buttered sandwich in the pan. "I don't know why you won't eat these. The bread is so crunchy, the peanut butter soft and melted."

"I don't know why you *do*. But then I never understood why you ate peanut butter and onion sandwiches in junior high."

"Isn't that sick? I don't know why I did either. But then I could never understand why you wore your bangs taped to your forehead on the way to school."

Carolyn wiped the mayonnaise onto her bread. "I had to have perfect hair. I hated my curls, and demanded that at least one part of my hair be tamed."

"You always had to be in control, didn't you?"

Carolyn nodded. "And you always needed to follow the right leader. Do you think we'll ever change?"

Joann flipped her sandwich. "I think I have."

"Are you in control now?" Carolyn asked, doubting.

"I don't know if you could say I'm in control. I think I don't jump to conclusions or blindly follow the leader anymore. I have made some pretty strong decisions, especially in the past year." Joann wanted so much to share with Carolyn about Ross. She wanted someone to be proud of her for the steps she was taking to leave the past behind, to love, honor, and cherish her husband, and her husband only. She wanted someone to be proud of the way she fought thoughts that crept into her mind. Thoughts that tempted her to compare David with Ross, and find David lacking. She had won over the thoughts of comparison she made at first when they made love. But she had won, and she never thought of Ross anymore when she and David were in bed together. She wanted to share the laughter and good times she and Ross had had together. But she would never be able to share them with anyone. Their relationship was a secret from the beginning, and always would be. She fought the secret that festered and grew, begging to be shared, threatening to burst through at times. Like when she smelled eucalyptus trees. She wanted to tell about the time she and Ross had a picnic in a circle of them, the smell pungent. She could remember everything they said, every kiss, every caress, each time she smelled those trees.

She and Ross laughed again over the movie they had seen the night before. And then he had asked her to marry him . . . someday, right there, in that circle of trees. She had never felt so loved, so beautiful, so wanted.

"I'm glad to hear you can stand on your own two feet," Carolyn said, dropping the knife into the sink. "I didn't want to play follow the leader here in River Edge too."

The remark stung even though it wasn't meant to. Joann scooped her sandwich from the pan, putting it on a blue Corelle dish. Carolyn never used Corelle.

"Milk?" Carolyn asked, pulling the carton from the refrigerator.

"Punch," Joann replied.

"Punch? For a growing baby?"

"Okay, milk."

"I thought you made your own decisions."

Joann smiled. "I do, unless I'm wrong."

Carolyn settled into her chair. "Do you feel like you've been on an emotional seesaw today?"

Joann chewed her gooey sandwich, nodding.

"Me too. I guess from what I hear, *you'd* better get used to it. My friends have told me it's like being on a roller coaster for nine months."

"Wonderful. That means I've got six months left."

"Then come postpartum blues."

"Does it ever end?"

"When the kids leave home."

They both laughed. Joann said, "So what's your excuse for riding the seesaw."

"The subjects of conversation."

The rest of the day passed in catching up on the little things of life that had taken place since the last time they had been together before the move. With good friends, Joann realized, the passing of time is nonexistent. The friendship takes up where it left off. The lack of communication is simply a nuisance.

When the last nail had been hammered into the wall, Joann stepped to the middle of the living room, turning slowly around. "Carolyn, the apartment looks fabulous!"

"Thanks."

"Now I feel like I'm really home."

Carolyn smiled as she pulled the keys to her Camaro from her purse. "I'm glad. Hey, do you and David want to go on a picnic next weekend?"

"I don't know yet. We won't know David's schedule until tomorrow."

"Don't you hate not knowing until the last minute?"

"Of course, but that's the way the grocery business is. As soon as David works his way up in the produce department, then his hours and days off will be consistent. But then he will have to work Sundays, too."

"Why'd he ever choose such a yucky business to get into?"

Joann shrugged. "He loves it."

"I'd better get going."

"Thanks!" Joann waved as Carolyn hopped in her car and took off for home.

Joann put her Mexican TV dinner in the oven, then turned on the television. Going into the room of the loved and future child, she dug around in the boxes until she found the fabric scraps she wanted, the colored quilting threads, and some batting. Curled up on the couch, she began to create as she waited for her dinner to cook.

·5·

··Davidknocked on the door three times before using his key to let himself in. Joann looked like a small child, rolled up in a little ball on the couch, asleep. Her chestnut hair fell over her face. Her hands curled under it, pushing her features out of shape. An ancient green TV tray stood watching a sitcom family argue as canned laughter filled the air. A tin plate sat on top of the tray, cleaned out except for half of the refried beans. A glass with three swallows of milk remaining sat beside it.

It made David angry to walk into his house and see garbage left out, especially since they had a constant battle with ants. He also felt compassion for his exhausted wife.

He hadn't loved her the moment he saw her sitting alone on the beach. David only saw her loneliness, and wanted to draw the shy girl into the crowd, to make her feel like she belonged.

After the first hour of talking with her, he knew he wanted to get to know her better. She had such strong opinions about life, and her goals were reasonable and clear. What drew him the most were her eyes. He noticed something behind them that touched his heart. She needed a friend, someone to talk to, someone to share her pain.

It took him a whole year to realize he loved her, and wanted her to be his wife. It took another six months to convince her she loved him too.

Being married to her wasn't heaven on earth, it was real. Fights and arguments, passion and caring, fun and boredom. He had grown tired of asking about the undercurrent of pain in her life. She never shared it. She often said, "David, if I hurt somehow, I'd tell you. I'm as happy as can be."

David hated the lie, but gave up trying to discover the source. He decided if he loved her enough to commit his life to her, he could forget his need to know the secret.

He reached out to brush the hair away from her nose and mouth, then went into the bedroom to change out of his work clothes.

"David, is that you?" Joann called out sleepily.

"Yeah, babe," he said, pulling a blue and gold striped T-shirt over his head. He walked out of the bedroom, watching as Joann stretched, then got up to clean her mess.

"Want anything to eat?"

"No thanks." He followed her into the kitchen, turning her around to kiss her.

Joann smiled, her arms wrapped around his neck. "Carolyn came by today to help hang pictures."

David kissed her again, then put his arm around her waist, walking back to the living room. "I noticed. It looks nice. I'm glad she helped."

"Me, too. She is so busy these days. I'm disappointed I don't get to see more of her."

"Maybe you should join whatever it is she is doing. Have you found out what it is yet?"

Joann folded up the TV tray. "She's working for some committee against abortion."

David flopped on the couch. "Ooh, hot topic. Good cause. Have you thought about joining? You could meet people, make new friends, and be working for something worthwhile at the same time."

"No, I hadn't thought about it," she said, her voice cool.

"Maybe you should," he insisted.

"Maybe I shouldn't. Can you imagine a pregnant lady around those clinics?" Joann flopped next to him, cuddling close, under his arm.

"Who better to make a point?"

"Well, I don't think it's proper. Besides, I have too much to do before the baby comes."

"Like what?"

"Like making wall hangings, finishing the quilt, hooking a rug, making bumper pads. . . ."

"You can buy some of those things, you know."

"But I want everything to match."

David pulled back to study her face. "Why is that so important?"

"Our baby deserves the best, that's why."

"And store-bought, or gifts from friends just isn't good enough."

"Oh, David, stop. It's our first baby, and I want everything to be just right."

David took his arm from her shoulder, turning to face her. "Sometimes I wonder about this baby. It's already taking over our house and it isn't even here yet. I can't even tell you're pregnant yet. And who's to say this one's going to make it?"

Joann's eyes filled with tears. "Sometimes I think you don't want to have this baby." She started to get up from the couch.

David reached for her hand, pulling her back. He took both her hands, then looked right into her eyes. "I want a baby. I want several children. But we never discussed this decision. You never gave me a choice. Not this time, not the last. Having a baby is an obsession with you. And that scares me."

Joann turned away. "I'm not obsessed."

"You are."

"So you don't want this baby? You want me to get rid of it?" her voice became thin and high, piercing the air.

David threw his hands up. "Of course not. I only want you to back up a bit and see your craziness about it all. You have a husband too, remember me? Or am I just a legal machine to produce babies for you?"

Joann came out of her snit with a start. "Oh, no, David. I love you. I assumed you wanted babies right away like me. We did talk about children a lot before we were married."

David remembered those conversations. Lots of them. Joann loved to talk about her children, what they would be like, what she would do with them, and what they would all do together as a family. He always loved the way Joann handled children. He enjoyed the conversations for a while. Then he tired of them, trying to steer the conversation back to discussing their relationship.

He put his arm around her, pulling her close. "We talked about children a lot before we were married. But the timing was never mentioned."

Joann looked at the floor. "I just assumed. . . ."

"Next big decision, consult me first, okay? It's my life too. We did agree to share our lives, not let one person steamroll the other." David kissed the top of her head, to show her there was no resentment or anger. He hoped she understood since he couldn't tell her.

The road to Highland Springs cut through orchards and farms, making it seem farther away than seven miles. The car bumped over the dusty road that dropped down the side of the hill.

"Hey, this is a lake!" David exclaimed. "When I think of springs, I think of pond. So I never bothered to come out here. This is great."

Rob parked the car in the weeds. Carolyn jumped out with her set of car keys, popping open the trunk. She stuffed each set of arms full of something, then guided the group to the spot she liked best. A large oak tree spread its branches like a canopy, to shield some of the sun, but not all of it. "The temperature here is perfect," she explained.

David shaded his eyes, looking over the lake. "The reeds are so thick. How do you get to the water?"

"There's a spot around the corner over there," Rob pointed, "where the reeds don't grow. There's a rope swing over there too."

David pulled his shirt off his muscular body. "Great, I'm ready, are you?"

Rob looked around, making certain no one watched as he took off his shirt. "Yes, how about you ladies?"

"You bet!" Carolyn said.

"I'll wade," Joann insisted. "I'm not taking any chances."

Carolyn handed Joann a towel, tucked one under her own arm, and the two followed the men across the sharp grass.

Carolyn joined the line of jumpers, watching Joann choose a rock to sit on and watch. Joann had changed since high school, Carolyn thought. She had, too, but she felt hers was more of a maturity, whereas Joann's change seemed to be in her personality. Something had changed her from being a happy, bouncy person into someone serious with some strange ideas. *Maybe that's what pregnancy does to you,* she thought.

The rope swing creaked as the kids in line let out Tarzan yells, swinging free of the earth, then dropping like bombs into the water. David ran off the edge, swinging out farther than the rest. He let out a whoop, and flailing in midair, he tried to stay up as long as possible. Carolyn laughed, and noticed Joann had covered her face, and shook her head. Joann looked up to see Carolyn looking at her. "He's still a kid!" she yelled.

Carolyn laughed again and nodded. Ramrod Rob went into the water as straight as he dropped from the rope. Emerging from the water, he stated in a quiet voice, "Fun, great fun."

Carolyn shook her head this time, calling to Joann. "I don't think Rob ever was a kid."

Carolyn grabbed the rope, the fibers pricking into her hands. As she swung out, the air blew into her face, and the fun, scary feeling fluttered in her stomach. She dropped into the water with a tiny splash. As she swam to shore, little fish nipped at her legs. When she got out, David was pulling Joann by the arm. "Come on, Jo. It's great fun. You'll be okay."

Joann looked frightened. "No, David. Please don't."

Carolyn touched David's shoulder. "Leave the poor lady alone," she teased. "If she doesn't want to have any fun, let her be."

David dropped Joann's arm. "I'll make up for you," he said.

Carolyn rode the swing three more times before she sat on the edge of the rock with Joann. "Will you at least swim to the raft with me?"

Joann looked pleased. "Of course. I'm getting tired of watching everyone else have fun."

Carolyn waited while Joann hoisted herself up the ladder, then followed her. Carolyn lay on the warm wood, facing her. She propped her chin on her hands. "Do you like it up here?"

"At Highland Springs?"

"Northern California, I mean. Lake Ridge specifically."

"Three weeks isn't much time to judge, but I think I do. It's so quiet, and beautiful. There is certainly nowhere in L.A. that you can drive seven miles and be out in the country. I'm also tired of the craziness of living in L.A."

"You'll find the good outweighs the bad here."

The sun dried the water off Carolyn's back. The raft rocked her, until she was about to fall asleep.

Joann spoke softly. "Do you ever think about the first man you ever loved?"

"Man? Brad was hardly a man. But yes, I do. I think about him sometimes when things happen to remind me of him. Brut aftershave, the movies we saw together."

"I think of mine, too. I feel bad about it."

Carolyn thought Joann's voice sounded timid and full of guilt. "I don't think you can ever forget someone you loved. I don't think you need to, either, unless you think of him in ways that could get you in trouble."

"Like wanting things to be the way they used to be?"

Carolyn laid her cheek on her hands and closed her eyes. "Mmhmm. Wanting hugs, kisses, all that wonderful romance. Wanting the good things from him, forgetting the balance of bad memories."

"What if there are no bad memories?"

Carolyn propped her head up on her chin again. "No bad memories? You must not have had a realistic relationship."

Joann didn't answer. Her head was down, her eyes closed. Carolyn closed her eyes, remembering that first love. She still wondered what had happened to him, but she didn't ever want to trade him for Rob. Rob slipped into her life, unnoticed, her senior year in college.

She worked part time in the accounting office as assistant to the secretary. She hated the job, but it gave her some money to help pay for the expensive education her parents financed. She paid no attention to the stuffy accountants who wandered in and out of the office all day; wearing three-piece suits, carrying briefcases, they looked like clones of one another. She might never have noticed Rob if it wasn't for the quarterly report she had to help him finish. All the numbers drove her crazy.

In the middle of the final page, Carolyn tried to concentrate, to get it done before the deadline. In marched Rob, holding out three pages she had completed the day before. "Did you type these?" he asked.

Perturbed, she grabbed them from his hand, looked at them, then handed them back. "Yes, I did. I'm on the last one now."

The papers fluttered to her desk. "You've got three more after that one."

Carolyn stopped her typing and looked into his face. "What are you talking about?"

She noticed his jaw muscles bulging as he cracked his knuckles. "You didn't get all the numbers correct on the pages. I marked the correct numbers in pencil."

"Good, then I can use White-out on the wrong ones."

Rob stood up straighter. "You may not. No correcting fluid. No ink marks, no pencil marks. You must retype them number perfect."

Carolyn fumed as he walked away. She retyped the pages, grumbling over each one. Before leaving them on his desk, she typed a cryptic note. "Remind me never to be your private secretary." The next day, a note sat on her desk. "Remind me never to hire you."

By the end of the week, they were laughing over the notes they left on each other's desks, and soon they were dating. They were married a year later.

Carolyn smiled. She loved Rob. He might not laugh much, but his dry sense of humor kept her laughing. She wondered why he didn't let that humor show, or why he laughed only around certain people.

The rocking and the warm sun coaxed her to sleep, thinking of Rob's support for her in all her crazy and not-so-crazy endeavors. He never understood her, but he supported her.

* * *

Drops of cold water and Joann's shrieks woke her. "What do you think you guys are doing?" she asked Rob and David.

"We wanted to eat, but you two were here snoozing away the afternoon," David said.

Carolyn shaded her eyes, looking up at them. "And you two poor boys are unable to serve yourselves?"

"We served ourselves," David replied. "We thought you would want to know we ate all the food."

Joann stood up and looked him right in the eye. She turned to Carolyn. "He's lying."

David smiled. "Never marry a woman who knows you. It's dangerous and no fun." David kissed her.

"David, don't. Everyone can see."

"Why? Don't you want the world to know what a handsome husband you have?"

"Oh, David," she shoved him away, seeming to enjoy his silliness. *Joann always loved teasing and playing games,* Carolyn thought. It seemed so childish now.

"Let's race," David shouted as he dove off the platform. Joann motioned for them to wait. Carolyn watched David's strong strokes pull him toward shore. He stood up in waist-high water, turning to look for the rest of them.

Joann shouted, "You won!" then dove in, taking her time to reach shore, with Carolyn and Rob following close behind.

Carolyn set up the food in the center of the blanket.

"You can sure tell who made this lunch," quipped David as he piled his plate with carrots, celery, olives, and fruit salad. He stuffed cheese wedges next to the carrots and sprinkled assorted nuts anywhere he could find a space.

Carolyn smiled at the compliment. "Why do you think I asked Joann to bring cookies? She has so much talent for junk food, she doesn't know what good eating is."

Joann stuck her tongue out at them, then popped an olive into her mouth. "I just enjoy the pleasures of eating. You, on the other hand, eat to get healthy."

Joann watched one group of high-school kids having a water-balloon fight. Another group played softball, another horseshoes. Carolyn leaned over to whisper to her. "Want to go play?"

Joann smiled. "Why do we have to be too old to do that kind of stuff?"

"Somebody like Rob must have written the rules."

Carolyn cleaned up the remnants of lunch, and served Joann's cookies. Joann took two, then handed six to David.

He leaned over to kiss her, and Rob groaned. "If you guys don't quit that, Carolyn will be asking me to kiss her. I couldn't tolerate that."

Carolyn smiled. "I wouldn't think of embarrassing you like that, Rob. I'd rather embarrass you in other ways."

·7·

The teddy bear responded to Joann's hug. The soft smell of cedar mixed with twenty years of dust brought with it memories of sadness and comfort. Of two skinned knees at five, when she tried to learn to ride her bike without training wheels, and couldn't. Of the movie she wanted to see so bad, but her parents told her it "compromised" their beliefs—whatever *compromise* meant to a nine-year-old. Of staying at Aunt Mindy's house, and wanting to go home and sleep in her own bed. But Mom and Dad had gone away to a "retreat" until Sunday.

Now Teddy, his eyes and nose long gone, his head flopping over, shared her undefined pain. The longing that could not be fulfilled, the pain that could never be fixed. It hurt too bad. But Teddy knew. He hugged her back.

When Joann got him that Christmas, she held him all day. He was almost as big as she was, and became her very best friend.

She cried when her sister slugged him. She whispered that it was "for his own good" when she shoved him into a trunk to protect him.

His oversized ears heard all her secrets, and never betrayed her confidence. So he knew her deepest, most painful secret. The worst secret. A necessary deed. He knew the dichotomy of the secret. The teddy knew, because Joann had told him that what she did was right. And what she did was eternally wrong.

Joann wondered if he pondered these things as he slouched in the corner.

The key in the front door startled her, and Teddy landed in the corner, his soft body a reddish lump.

"What've you been up to, babe?" David asked after they shared a hello kiss.

"Fixing up the baby's room a bit. Why are you home?"

"You sound unhappy about it."

"Just surprised, that's all."

"I thought I'd come home for lunch and a little dessert." His smile told her what dessert would be. Her smile matched his.

"So do you want dessert now or after lunch?"

"Now."

* * *

Joann opened the drapes. "I did hear a truck. Looks like we've got new neighbors."

David carried his sandwich to the window to observe the action. "From the looks of their furniture, they're probably about our age."

"I'll have to make some cookies and take them over tomorrow."

David nodded, chewing his last bite of sandwich. "My wife . . . Welcome Wagon for the Lakeside apartment complex."

"How better to make new friends?" She watched two men struggling with a dresser. "I think I'll make caramel chocolate squares."

"You can't do that. Those are my favorites."

"You can have one."

"One?"

"It's better than none."

"You sound like my mother."

"Watch it, buster."

* * *

Joann balanced the plate of gooey bars on one hand as she knocked on the door. A young woman in her midtwenties answered the door, her long black hair pulled back, tied with a scarf. "Hi."

46

"Hi. I'm Joann Simpson, your neighbor in number four. I thought you might like some homemade goodies to snack on while you unpack."

"How thoughtful of you. My name's Teresa Meyer." She turned her head and called, "Dan, come here and meet one of our neighbors."

A man appeared from behind a pile of boxes. "I'm Dan," he said with a warm smile.

Joann tried not to stare at who she felt was probably the second ugliest man in the world. His blond stringy hair limped across his face, his black glasses were so out of style, she hadn't seen anyone wear that kind since junior high school. And somehow, they managed to clash with his hair. Black pores clustered on his white, chubby face.

He reached for the plate Joann offered. "This is the nicest welcome we've ever had, isn't it, Teresa?" He looked at Joann. "How we got the best apartment, I'll never know. But you can use the deck anytime you wish."

"Why, thank you. I've been envious of the lucky people who got this apartment. I love looking at the lake."

Dan pushed his hair back into place. "I've got to get back to work, after I revive myself with one of these. Thank you very much."

"Yes, Joann," Teresa added. "Thank you for your kindness. I hope I can repay you sometime."

Joann waved away the offer, then made one of her own. "If you need anything at all, please come knock on our door. I've finally learned where all the crucial stores are, so just ask. You can use our telephone, too, until you get yours. Anything. Just ask."

Joann felt like skipping back to her apartment, but traded who she wanted to be for who others thought she should be, and walked instead, compromising with a bit of a bounce.

* * *

The knock came, two days later. "I'm sorry to bother you, Joann, but may I use your phone?"

"Of course!" Joann said, happy her offer had been taken seriously.

"I need to call the phone company. I thought they'd have our phone line ready by now."

"Here? In Lake Ridge? It took us two weeks to get a number. I guess they don't have enough lines. Here's the phone, and here's the number of the phone company."

Joann curled her feet underneath her on the sofa, and went back to work on the Bible-study lesson the knock had interrupted. Her thoughts were so focused, she didn't hear Teresa come into the room. "What are you doing?" Teresa asked.

The question so startled Joann, the "t" she was writing took flight on the page. She looked up. "A Bible-study lesson."

Teresa sat on the opposite end of the couch. "What are you studying?"

"Colossians."

"My favorite book."

Surprised, Joann asked, "Are you a Christian?"

Teresa smiled. "Yes. I was hoping you might be. Dan and I want to find a good church right away."

"Come with us on Sunday."

"Okay. When's the Bible study?"

"Tuesdays at nine thirty."

"Can I try that too?"

"Of course. I'm pretty new there myself. We just moved here three months ago."

"You sure you don't mind my tagging along?"

"It would be fun. You can meet my friend Carolyn too."

"Good. See you Sunday then?"

✻ ✻ ✻

Sunday's rain altered their plans to walk along the lakeshore to church. Afterward they drove to the Water Wheel Cafe for lunch. Carolyn and Rob invited themselves along.

Rob shut his menu, putting it on the corner of the table. "What brings you two to Lake Ridge?" he asked.

"Probably the same thing that brought you," Dan replied. "Small town, the beauty, getting away from the craziness of the city."

"No kidding," David agreed.

"What kind of work do you do?" Rob asked.

"I'm a mailman," Dan replied.

They all stared, and tried to look like they weren't.

Dan continued. "I chose the job because I love being out-of-doors. Lake Ridge seemed like a pretty enough place to be out-of-doors a lot. Besides, they had an opening."

Everyone laughed.

David asked, "What do you like most about your work? I have to admit, it seems like a boring job to me."

"It can be. But I spend the time praying for the people I know. Missionaries, friends, about world events, and so on. I know I'll never make much money to do or buy wonderful things, but my prayers can be how I touch people and help them."

The admiration in Teresa's dark eyes was obvious. This ugly man had a heart of gold. *No wonder she loves him*, Joann thought.

The waitress mixed up the lunch orders. As soon as she left, the strays were passed to the rightful eaters. "Typical Lake Ridge service," Rob said as everyone sipped their drinks to find Joann's root beer.

Eating slowed the conversation at first, until the initial hunger pangs were satisfied.

"How do you feel about abortion?" Carolyn asked Teresa, before tucking away a mouthful of chef's salad. The group looked stunned, except Teresa.

"Why don't we talk about that later," Teresa said. "I'd rather find out where you're from."

A standing ovation went on in Joann's mind. *This is my kind of friend.*

The group couldn't seem to end their conversation, even when the after-meal cups of coffee had dried in the bottom of the mugs. They might have been there until evening if David hadn't rescued a drooping Joann. "These pregnant ladies sleep their lives away," he said. "I'd better get her home for her nap."

Joann tried to look ugly, but only succeeded in looking more tired. The new friends parted with a date for Trivial Pursuit and popcorn at Carolyn and Rob's house.

In the car, Joann turned to Teresa. "Thanks for diverting the conversation during lunch. Abortion isn't my favorite mealtime discussion."

"Don't thank me. I did it for myself."

David talked to Dan over his shoulder. "Well, we sure talked about a variety of topics over lunch. Where did you learn so much?"

Dan shrugged his shoulders. "Teresa tells me to say I read people's mail. Really I'm just curious, so I ask a lot of questions."

"And he never forgets the answers," Teresa added. "It's a marvelous gift, this combination of interest in others, and excellent memory. He's a born conversationalist."

Dan blushed, pushing his stringy hair in place, where it stayed as long as his hand held it there.

"No wonder you love the guy," Joann said.

Teresa held her hand up to her mouth, shielding it from Dan. "Just don't let him know that."

Dan looked uncomfortable. Teresa smiled and spoke for him. "His only fault is that he hasn't much of a sense of humor. I guess his compassion runs too deep."

Joann thought Dan looked like he'd rather be invisible. "Teresa, please don't," he whispered. "You know. . . ."

"I know." Teresa kissed his cheek, which brought out a full blush. They stood talking under the carport for another five minutes, before dashing through the downpour to their apartments.

Joann felt comfortable and happy as she lay down for her nap, and woke feeling the same way. It didn't bother her that David had left for work while she slept. She waved at blind Teddy as she walked to the living room to turn on an old movie. She glanced at it enough to keep track of the characters. Most of the time she paid attention to the rocking horse taking shape beneath her skillful needle.

She loved old movies. She loved happy endings. It comforted her to know that true love always won, and so did the good guy. Evil never triumphed, and the foolish choices made by people were never so awful that the good outcome would be destroyed.

Joann waited up until David came home at 11:00 P.M., the news creating a distracting background to their conversation. "Carolyn came in," David said. "She wants you to call her in the morning."

"Why doesn't she call me?"

"She said she's tired of waking you up. She seemed a little edgy."

"That's normal. How'd work go?"

"Same. I'm glad to be working under Mr. Saito, though. He's the perfect man to learn from. His father had a small produce market in Japan. Their ways of marketing are subtle and beautiful. Our department is the best in the chain, even though it is the smallest."

Joann nodded, paying more attention to the news than to David. A commercial came on, and she turned to look at him. "That's what you really want, isn't it?"

"To have my own produce department? Yes. Perhaps someday, a produce market of some kind. Now I'm just trying to learn all I can from Mr. Saito."

"I should meet him. How come he's never there when I come in?"

"He works early. Come in before three tomorrow, and he'll be there."

* * *

Joann felt fat, not pregnant, the next afternoon as she held her hand out to shake that of the old Japanese man. His hands were rough, like David's, only with years more work to have cracked and stained them.

50

His hands, solid and strong, quick in their movements, seemed incompatible with his thin, frail-looking body.

Mr. Saito looked with satisfaction at Joann's figure as they were introduced. "It is always a blessing to see new life."

Joann blushed, and said, "Thank you."

"Your David, he is my best worker."

David said, "Well, it is because you are such a good teacher, Mr. Saito."

"I think David has an eye for the work," Mr. Saito told Joann, "as well as a love for the produce. He will go far."

Joann watched as the hands of the two skillful men continued their work, building battlements of oranges. She saw, for the first time, David's intensity as he worked.

"The customers, they love your husband too," Mr. Saito said as he moved toward the lettuce. "He shares his knowledge with them, they choose the best, then they return because they think we have the best produce in town. He is good, very good."

It felt good to see David doing so well, and enjoying his work. Joann realized she had never paid attention, or even cared about the little things of David's job. She had often been embarrassed to tell people what he did. Thoughts of pride flowed as she wandered through the store, choosing a few needed items. She followed her cart back to produce to say good-bye to David. A group of teenage girls stood around him, teasing and laughing. She hated the forced giggling, an obvious gesture to be noticed. David smiled at them, cordial, happy to trade the banter. "No wonder he likes this shift," Joann said to herself. "He can play all he wants." Joann whirled around and marched out of the store, leaving her basket behind.

*   *   *

"Why did you leave without saying good-bye this afternoon?"

Joann made sure her sarcasm would bite hard. "I came to say good-bye, but you were having so much fun, I hated to interrupt."

David looked confused, then a red flush began to creep up his face. "You have no right to judge."

"No wonder you don't wear a wedding ring," she shouted at him. She knew she should regret her words, but she didn't.

David's jaw started working like he was chewing gum as he stroked his mustache. "I've told you, the continuous contact with water causes infections underneath it."

"I used to believe that."

"*And,*" David continued, his anger swelling, "it has gotten caught on the crates a couple of times, and almost yanked my finger off."

"Handy arguments."

"So Miss Perfect, where's your ring?"

Joann covered her left hand. Her voice was soft as she made her feeble, but true, argument. "You know the doctor told me to take it off. My hands are swelling a little bit, and might cause problems later in the pregnancy."

"You see what you are doing? Anything that has to do with *baby* is okay. It is okay for you not to wear your ring, but you will accuse me when I can't wear mine. I'm tired of coming home in the evenings to talk about the baby moving and doctor's visits. My work and my life are unimportant to you until you have something to complain about."

"That's not true," Joann protested, knowing it *was* true.

"We've been here almost three months, and today is the first time you made an effort to watch me work. That hurts, Jo. Why is it that you can be so wrapped up in yourself, and never let me in? I feel like there is a wall around some secret castle you've built."

In a high-pitched voice, Joann said, "I don't have any secrets from you."

David, his anger spent, said, "I don't have any secrets from you either." He buried her head in his shoulder. "There is no one in my life but you."

And there is no one in my life except you—and Ross, Joann thought, the guilt swelling up, choking her.

David wrapped his arms around Joann, and Joann felt the baby kick him. She opened her mouth to tell him, then kissed him instead.

"My goodness, Joann, what happened to you?" Carolyn asked.

"What do you mean?" Joann said, holding the phone with her shoulder, her arms elbow deep in dishwater.

"In high school you were the most outspoken person I knew. You didn't hesitate to tell anyone what they were doing was wrong and stupid. I remember you telling Yvonne how ugly she looked when she smoked! No one dared talk to Yvonne, and you told her she was ugly!"

Joann chuckled at the memory. "Everyone thought she'd slug me, but she didn't."

"She was too shocked to do anything. My point is, you were so against drugs, drinking, and sex, not only for yourself, but everybody else too. You were the only kid I knew who refused to go to victory parties. So why are you so wishy-washy now?"

Joann sighed. "I have always been wishy-washy, a follower."

"Yes, but you still had strong convictions. You chose a leader who shared those convictions. It's that strength you've lost. You have no backbone."

Joann thought a moment. "Maybe I've just gained compassion."

"Compassion? Standing by silently while the world kills all the little babies they don't want is not compassion."

Joann tried to keep her voice calm. "Carolyn, trust me. I'm as much against abortion as you are. I just think there's another side to it, that's all."

"Another side? Joann, you're impossible! The only other side is disgusting. Selfish people doing horrible things."

"Yes, Carolyn, you've said that before. You have to look at—"

"The only thing to look at are the pictures of those poor massacred babies. All that life thrown in the garbage!" Carolyn's voice filled with emotion, a tender anger. "Have you ever looked at those pictures?"

Joann's chest tightened, her voice reflecting the tightness. "No."

"What? No wonder you aren't convinced. You must come with me to a movie two weeks from Thursday at the pro-life center. You'll never doubt again."

Joann hesitated. "Okay," she said, knowing she would never go. She could not have lied successfully if Carolyn had been there. It would have shown in her eyes. "Make sure you give me the details."

Carolyn's voice sounded victorious. "I'll bring a flyer over tomorrow after I do my grocery shopping."

"Fine. See you then."

Joann hung up, thoughts racing. The phone rang the minute she stuck her hands back into the soapy water. She dried them before answering. Teresa gave Joann her new phone number, and Joann invited her over to visit, a buffer, she hoped, when Carolyn came the next day. "Can you come for lunch?"

"Great. Shall I bring my own?"

"My reputation spreads fast, doesn't it?" Joann said, laughing. "No, I'll have real food."

* * *

The next day, Joann made a lunch of barbecued beef sandwiches from a leftover roast.

Teresa wiped her mouth and pushed the empty plate away from her. "You can cook, can't you?" she teased.

"See if I ever invite you for lunch again."

"This heat up here is killing me," Teresa said. "I'm glad you believe in using your air conditioner."

"I couldn't live without it. I can't believe people come to Lake Ridge because they enjoy the heat."

"Carolyn said August is worse. We have three more days to enjoy July."

Joann cleared the table. "Want a chocolate-chip cookie?"

"Always." She pulled her long hair over one shoulder, then took a cookie from the can.

Carolyn waltzed in, carrying a bag of grapes. "Teresa! I'm glad you're here. I can give you one of these things too."

"Grapes?"

"Grapes and . . . didn't Joann tell you? I want her to come see a movie on abortion in a couple of weeks. I think she needs a little convincing on the subject. No one should straddle the fence like that. Not on such an important issue."

"I agree with that," Teresa said. "I'd be interested in what your group has to say."

Carolyn helped herself to a bowl from Joann's cupboard, shaking the grapes into it, then sticking them under the water to wash them. "I hoped you might be interested. To tell you the truth, we need more workers."

Teresa held up her hand. "I don't know if I can be a worker, but I am interested in seeing the movie. No pressure, okay?"

"Fair enough."

I wish she'd be fair with me, Joann thought.

Carolyn set the washed grapes on the kitchen table. She plucked a few and popped them in her mouth, one at a time. "Help yourself."

She opened her purse, pulled out two pamphlets, and put them on the table. She said to Joann, "Who is that cute little high-school girl I saw talking to David in the store?"

"Which one?" Joann asked, trying to sound casual.

Teresa perked up. "You mean the one with the thick blonde braid that goes down to the top of her jeans? Hazel eyes, kind of chubby?"

"That's the one. You can hear her giggle an aisle away. Know which one now, Joann?"

Joann stared at the grapes she pulled from the cluster. "I can't place her."

"She would be hard to miss. I've seen her tease everyone in the store. When she laughs, her whole body laughs with her," Carolyn added.

"Good for her," Joann said.

Teresa came to the girl's defense. "She seems like a nice kid."

"I bet she'd be a good sitter for little no-name in there," Carolyn said, tapping Joann's stomach.

"I don't think I'll need a sitter. I plan to take the baby with us wherever we go."

Carolyn looked at Teresa and rolled her eyes. "I bet you change your mind," she said to Joann. "When you do, I'll baby-sit for you."

"Don't look at me," Teresa said. "I don't have any kids yet, because they aren't my specialty. So as backup, you'd better find out who this girl is."

"I can't stand the thought of being away from the baby for any length of time," Joann said.

"Okay, so don't find out. I think she's a real nice girl," Carolyn said. "I better get my groceries home before the frozen yogurt melts."

Teresa read the advertisement for the movie, popping grapes into her mouth one at a time. "Are you going to go?"

"I don't think so."

"It sounds informative. I'm interested in hearing facts, but look, it says here, 'graphic scenes shown.' I don't need that."

"Me neither."

"Carolyn's really pushing you, isn't she?"

Joann nodded. "I think it's because we have been friends for so long. She wants my interests to be the same as hers. She always has."

"A twisted sort of compliment."

"I never saw it that way before. I guess that's true. She enjoys our being together." Joann stuck another grape in her mouth, thinking as she chewed. "You know, I think it's hard for her to see our energies being spent on different things."

"Maybe she would leave you alone if you went with her once."

Joann shook her head. "I don't think it would work. I think she'd be on me more than ever."

"I disagree. Isn't it worth a try?"

Joann looked into Teresa's eyes. "I really don't want to go."

"What will you tell Carolyn?"

"I don't know."

Joann's mind searched and discarded all the possibilities for excuses over the next four hours. Nothing short of lying or faking a disease seemed to be the answer, and those wouldn't work either. The spinning thoughts drove her crazy. Tired of pacing the house, she touched up her makeup, changed her clothes, and went for a walk.

The warm evening air refreshed her. She strolled along, stopping at times to watch the boats fly past. The towed skiers cut through the water, creating rooster tails that shot into the air, a watery screen between her and the skier.

Joann loved the lake and its moods. Sometimes it was agitated gray, choppy and foreboding. Sometimes, a peaceful blue, smooth as glass. Tonight, the water was a choppy, excited blue with hundreds of boats and skiers on its surface. Joann reluctantly left it behind for the grocrey store. On the way, she stopped to make friends with a neighbor watering his yard, and an old lady walking in the other direction. *I love the friendliness of the people in this town*, she thought.

* * *

"What are you doing here?" David asked, after kissing her cheek.

"I thought we'd kill the monotony of our routine and get an ice cream cone somewhere as soon as you're off."

"Okay, I have about five more minutes of work in the back."

Ten minutes later they walked hand in hand along the row of shops, pushing open the door of the brightest one.

The hot fudge slid down the Mount Everest of ice cream. "Are you sure you can eat all that?" David asked.

"Of course," Joann said, shoveling in a mouthful as proof.

"Did Carolyn come by?" David asked, chopping off a piece of banana to eat with his strawberry ice cream.

"Yes. After lunch. Teresa was over too."

"What did Carolyn want?"

"She wants me to go to an abortion movie with her."

"When is it?"

"A week from Thursday."

David looked disappointed. "Are you going to go?"

"I doubt it."

The disappointment turned to relief. "I found out I have that day off," David told her. "Joe wanted to trade days off with someone, and I agreed. I thought we'd drive to Mendocino."

"I'd like that."

"You won't be disappointed?"

"I'll bet she'll ask me again."

David laughed. "Carolyn is so dependable."

Joann scooped the fudge off the side of the dish, closing her eyes to taste it better. As she dipped her spoon for another bite, she said, "Carolyn told me about some little high-school girl she sees you talking with in the afternoons."

57

"Vicki?"

"Long braid, teases everyone."

"That's Vicki. She's lots of fun."

"I'll bet."

"Come on, Joann. She's a high-school kid. I think she's a little lonely. I've asked her to come over and meet you sometime. I told her about your quilting, and she said she's always wanted to learn."

Joann felt less threatened, knowing he had talked about her to Vicki. "I guess that would be okay."

"I'll send her over next week."

* * *

Joann rubbed the sleep from her eyes, shook her head, and ran her fingers through her hair, trying to look presentable for whoever was knocking at her door.

Opening the door, she saw a young girl, fitting the description of someone she was supposed to know, but couldn't remember through the cobwebs still tangling the sleepy brain cells.

"Hi, I'm Vicki," she said. "I hope I didn't catch you at a bad time."

Joann smothered a yawn. "No, not at all. Come in."

It was obvious Vicki did not feel self-conscious or rude looking around the room, staring at the walls as though she were in a museum. "Did you make all these?"

"Yes, I did."

"Don't sound so modest. These are terrific!"

"Thank you." Joann led Vicki around each room, describing each piece, and answering the myriad of questions Vicki had about them.

They stopped in the kitchen, where Joann pulled down the cookie can, and put it on the table beside the glasses of milk she had poured.

"Ooh, homemade chocolate chip. My favorite. I'm going to have to hang around you, I can tell. Would you teach me how to make all this stuff?"

"Which? The cookies or the quilting?"

"Both."

"Wouldn't your mother teach you?"

"She doesn't bake cookies. She drinks."

Vicki's unconcerned, matter-of-fact tone shook Joann. She didn't know what to do with the remark, so she let it slide. Vicki ate four cookies and gulped two glasses of milk before speaking again.

"David had told me you were pregnant. When's the baby due?"

"October."

"How far along does that make you?"

"Six. And bulging."

"What's it like to be pregnant?"

Joann felt strange answering that question. She wanted to say, "It depends on your situation." Instead, she said, "It's wonderful. My skin is pulling and stretching. . . ."

"And that's wonderful?"

"Mmmm. In a way. The baby is in there, growing, kicking, stretching. It is amazing to have that life in there. It's an awesome feeling, knowing there's a person waiting to come out and grow up in the world. I'm still amazed." *And sad.*

Vicki shook her head. "I can't imagine it either. But someday I'd like to have some kids, and raise them right. I think you learn from your parents' mistakes. I sure won't make the same ones."

"What mistakes won't you make?"

Vicki looked beyond the walls. "The ones they made," she said after a long silence.

Joann took a deep breath, and picked up the glasses. *It's time to change the subject.* "How old are you, Vicki?"

"Sixteen."

"So you'll be a junior this year?"

"No, a sophomore."

"Do I detect some anger about that?"

Vicki pushed her lips together before answering. "I guess. It's one of their mistakes."

"How? . . ." The look on Vicki's face cut her short. *Try again.* "Who's your best friend at school?"

"I don't have any friends."

"Vicki," Joann argued, "you've got to have friends."

"Well, I don't. I'm the kid everyone avoids."

"Will you be my friend?"

Vicki smiled, the gloomy mask lifted. "You mean it?"

"I do."

"You know, I just love your husband. He is the nicest guy at the store."

Joann felt her jealousy rising. "Oh?"

"Yeah. He's the only one that doesn't try to pick up on us girls. Some of the girls hate that, but I like it. I know a true friend when I see one."

Shame doused the flame of jealousy. "I'm glad."

"Me, too. Afternoons get so boring. There's nothing to do in this town."

"Why don't you come over sometime, I'll teach you how to quilt."

"And make chocolate-chip cookies too?"

"As soon as this can runs out." *Which won't be long if Vicki keeps showing up*, she thought.

"When do we start?"

"Tuesday afternoon? You can come Thursdays, too, if you want. Buy some fabric and some batting for whatever project you want to start on."

A change came over Vicki's face. "Maybe I'd better wait awhile before I start."

"Tell you what," Joann said, "I've got so many scraps, I'll bet we can find something in the boxes that you can use."

Vicki's face brightened again. "Oh, thank you. I'll see you next Tuesday then?"

Tuesday didn't come soon enough for either of them. It surprised Joann how much she anticipated the teaching time. She couldn't decide whether she was more excited about teaching Vicki or spending time with her. She understood why David liked her, and why Carolyn and Teresa had noticed her. She thanked David over and over for sending Vicki by. David laughed. "And you were so worried."

"I wasn't worried."

David only smiled in response.

*   *   *

Flour covered the kitchen like fine dust. Cookie dough flecks dotted the walls and the cook's shirt. Joann sat in a chair, her head in her hands. "Vicki," she pleaded. "Remember to keep the speed down."

Vicki chuckled and guffawed, laughing until tears poured down her cheeks. At one point, she sounded like a foghorn as she tried to breathe between laughs. "I'm sorry, Joann. No wonder my mom never wanted to teach me anything. I warned you, I'm a klutz."

Joann looked up at her. "I never believed it. Until now."

That sent Vicki into more fits of laughter.

Joann tried to restore order to the scene. "Is everything all mixed together?"

"All except the chocolate chips." She opened the bag, dumped them in, and started up the mixer.

"*No, Vicki.* Turn it off!"

Vicki looked sheepish. "What did I do?"

"You have to use a spoon. Otherwise you will chop up the chips into little bits."

"Oh, is that all?" With the chips stirred in, Vicki popped large globs into her mouth. "Vicki, you'll get sick."

"And it will be worth every minute."

Joann shook her head, wondering if she should try another lesson again, or tactfully back out. When the first tray of cookies came out of the oven, she changed her mind when she saw the pride on Vicki's face.

As she shoveled the cookies onto the cooling rack, she said, "Joann, on Thursday you'll teach me to quilt?"

"Not this week. David and I are going to Mendocino."

Vicki looked concerned. "That isn't an excuse, is it?"

Joann smiled. "No, it's not an excuse!"

* * *

Mendocino appeared, standing out on a finger of harsh, beautiful land. The wet wind sandblasted the homes shuddering on the coastal bluff. Cypress trees bent over like old men walking with canes, their backs in a permanent hunch from continued stress. Joann and David pointed and exclaimed over the many beautiful Victorian homes, the shanties and clapboard houses lining the streets.

Volkswagen buses and bugs groaned through their gears, their drivers lost somewhere in hippie time. Joann stared at the women milling around the post office. Their long hair, snarled by the wind, drifted over Indian gauze blouses and woven jackets. Jean skirts hung to their calves, their feet bare, in homemade sandals, or heavy hiking boots. The bearded men wore flannel Pendleton shirts, the tails hanging out over their jeans. Some wore their hair braided, others, ponytails. Few had hair trimmed somewhere around their ears. *The homes and people of this town are so like each other*, Joann thought. *Radical, out of place, in another time, bizarre, yet fitting.*

David drove to the end of one street and parked. They walked along a dusty footpath, which led between golden weeds. When they reached the edge of the bluff, Joann looked down the rocky cliffs that dropped to the violent sea. "No wonder everybody in Lake Ridge says they are going to the 'coast.' "

"It's nothing like Santa Monica beach, is it?" David asked.

Joann shook her head in disbelief. "There's no beach anywhere."

The wind pushed at them until Joann had enough. They walked back to the car, and drove the short distance to the center of town.

Joann felt a smug satisfaction as she stepped from the car. Carolyn had been so disappointed that Joann chose the trip to Mendocino rather than the movie. Joann had tried not to smile at the look on Carolyn's face. "Maybe next time," Carolyn said.

Joann shrugged her shoulders. "We'll see."

The baby rolled, kicked, and stretched as she and David browsed through the shops and art galleries, pulling at Joann's grief like an excellent puppeteer. She hated the unexpected grief the baby caused, stripping her of her occasional joy. It made her think of her other two babies. The ones she would never know. The ones who left before she had a chance to feel their life swirling and twirling happy dances inside her.

If only it had been different that first time. But her pregnancy would have destroyed everything and everyone. It would have destroyed her parents: Dad, an elder in the church, pillar of the community, Mom, a Bible-study teaching leader, always the model of perfect behavior. The fights they had at home were put away for a few hours of church attendance or public obligations. Joann couldn't ruin that perfect image for them. She couldn't ruin Ross's career. She couldn't ruin her witness to the kids at the continuation high school where she volunteered her time two afternoons a week.

I had no other choice, she screamed silently to her baby.

"Are you okay?" David asked. "You've been staring at that baby book a long time."

"It's nice, so different from any of the others I've seen." She lowered her voice to a whisper. "When I see something like this, I think of the other one, and it makes me sad."

"I know," David said, not understanding. "Do you want to buy the book?"

"No, we can't afford it anyway."

"But if it's special. . . ."

"It's not something I want to remember."

The baby stayed quiet the rest of the day. *Rocked to sleep with all the walking,* Joann thought gratefully. She forced her mind away from the ugly memories, trying to make new ones with the beauty that surrounded her.

When the wind died down, they returned to the bluff, sitting for a while on a rock, sharing their dreams—the kind that can only be shared when the setting is right, when nothing seems real and all seems a fantasy.

David shared his dream for a produce stand supplied by local farmers. He told Joann how he could sell home-canned jams and jellies. "Maybe we could have a small side room where you could sell your quilts and hangings too," he suggested.

"I'd like that," Joann said, dreaming of sitting in a chair, working, while children played at her feet, the older ones helping Daddy.

"You know what I'd like, David. I'd like to teach, too. Maybe a class through church, or even the junior college."

Joann noticed the rocks and benches were filling up, as people came from town, waiting for the sunset. Some sat in positions of meditation, others wrapped themselves in the arms of lovers. Parents held children, others sat alone, all were silent.

The sun hid behind the gray clouds which hung like a cap in the sky, trimmed with blue along the bottom edges. Then through a ragged tear in the cap, a handful of rays shot through the tear, reaching to the sky.

David put his arm around Joann's waist. She clasped her hands around his middle, resting her head on his shoulder.

The muted sun became a burnt orange disk, slipping through the thin slot between the horizon of sky and ocean, its glory not ending, merely transferring to another place.

When the last red-gold rim had disappeared, most of the audience turned, still without speaking, and walked back up the path toward town. Joann and David followed them, caught in the spell of wonder the consistency and beauty of God's creation weaves.

The spell did not break until they entered a small, muggy restaurant that reeked of fish. They declared the fresh clam chowder the best they had ever eaten, promised to return, then left their fantasies for the real life waiting at home.

·9·

·*T·he sun scorched the sidewalk and parking lot. Billy refused to wear his shoes and thus spent half his time doing a hot-foot dance on the pavement.

"Stay in the shade," Carolyn ordered like a scratched record.

"Stay in shade, stay in shade," Billy sang as he danced. He climbed on a bus bench, draped his legs over the back, and hung his head upside down. "Stay in the shade, stay in the shade!" he called to the shoppers who pushed loaded carts out of the store. He smiled at those going in, certain they obeyed him.

"Ma'am, may I talk with you a moment?" Carolyn said as she blocked an elderly woman's path. The woman leaned on her cane, cocked her head, ready to listen. "It is a sad point our country has come to," Carolyn proceeded, "getting rid of our unwanted children by allowing the crime of abortion to continue."

"Oh, yes," the woman agreed.

"We must do something about it, and I have a petition right here for you to sign. It states how you would like the Roe versus Wade decision reversed, and abortions outlawed once again."

The woman nodded, reaching for the pen to sign the paper. "Thank you very much, ma'am."

"Good luck to you. It's a good cause."

"Thank you." She turned to check on Billy. "Billy, don't look in that lady's sack, it isn't nice."

Billy smiled, his hand still buried in the startled woman's sack. "I want a cookie, Sissy."

Carolyn walked to the bench. "We'll get an ice cream later, Billy, okay?"

Billy jumped up and down on the bench seat, clapping his chubby hands. "Oh boy, ice cream. Can I have it now, Sissy?"

"No, Billy, Sissy has some more work to do, so you play, okay?"

Billy danced around in circles on the bench seat. "Sissy work, Billy play."

Carolyn smiled at the woman whose bag had been invaded. "I'm sorry Billy was rude. He doesn't always understand etiquette."

The woman grunted. "Seems to me he could be better trained. Must be eight years old."

"Ten, but he a Down's child."

"No excuse. Never any excuse for a misbehaved child."

"Again, ma'am, accept my apologies."

The woman grunted again, staring at Billy, who had turned Injun warrior. His war dance made the bench slats bounce.

"I'm passing around a petition against abortion. Would you be willing to sign?"

"Why should I?" the woman asked, still staring at Billy.

Flustered, Carolyn answered, "It's a crime to be eliminating so many precious children before they have a chance to live in this world."

"The world's overcrowed. Too many unwanted brats as it is." She looked Billy up and down as if he were a case in point.

"Each child is a precious gift . . ."

"Sure, to them that want 'em. To them that don't, they're only a burden." She turned and stared into Carolyn's eyes. "I had me an abortion some forty-three years ago. Best thing I ever did. Best thing the country ever did was make it so no one had to go to some dirty place to have it done."

"Just because—"

"My ride's here," the woman said, picking up her sack and walking away. Carolyn dropped to the bench and immediately had a lap full of Billy. She put one arm around him, while with the other she swiped away a stray piece of his black hair. She kissed Billy on the top of his head. "You *are* a precious gift, Billy."

Billy's head wobbled back and forth. "Precious gift, precious gift." He stopped, still as stone, watching a man use the pay phone. The minute the man replaced the receiver in its hook, the statue turned to lightning. Billy jammed his finger into the coin return, coming out empty-handed. His mouth turned down for a moment. He skipped over to Carolyn, who talked to another woman. He stood on her feet a moment, then trotted back to the bench again.

"I just don't know if I should sign," the woman said. "I would want an abortion if I knew my baby would be retarded. I mean, what kind of life is that for a kid? They can't do anything worthwhile."

As the woman rambled on, Carolyn stood straighter, her chin inching upward. She clenched her teeth, to avoid angry words from bursting through. The woman stopped. Carolyn smiled a slow, forced smile. "See my brother over there?"

The woman nodded. "I've been watching him. He's adorable."

"He's a Down's child. Retarded."

The woman froze, then gushed, "Oh, I'm so sorry, I'm terribly sorry, I didn't know, I didn't mean. . . ." She grabbed the clipboard and signed, muttering the rest of the way into the store.

Carolyn walked back and forth in front of the store four times before she could confront another person. Billy followed, mimicking her frown and quick steps. He didn't mean to be funny. He only felt Carolyn's anger and knew no other way to "help."

* * *

"In a minute, Billy. Wait 'til I'm done talking with this nice lady."

"Nice lady, nice lady. Sissy, I want my ice cream *now*."

"And, ma'am, just think, my darling baby brother wouldn't be here if a woman of pro-choice had been pregnant with him."

"Ice cream, now."

The woman took one look at Billy and signed.

Ice cream dripped off the cone and Billy's chin, spotting his red shirt. Carolyn focused on the men for a time—easy targets since they preferred to get in and out of the store quickly, without hassles. Signing was easier than arguing.

When Billy made the sticky mess complete, Carolyn decided they needed to go home.

Billy made regular appearances at the three grocery stores in town, as well as those in Morristown, during the month he visited Carolyn. Carolyn wanted to get as many signatures as she could, so she took Billy with her every day. Each of the four Saturdays were spent dancing on the bus bench outside the abortion clinic in Morristown. Old ladies appeared from time to time. As they waited for the bus, they asked him his name.

"If I were a bird," he'd whisper, flap his arms, jumping from the bench and "fly" to Carolyn for safety. "If I were a bird," he'd sing, flapping in frantic circles around her until the bus came and took the women away.

Sometimes he'd carry a sign Carolyn had made for him. He clapped his hands when he saw the pretty rainbow-colored letters, even though he couldn't read them. "Sissy, what's it say?" he asked the first day.

Carolyn knelt beside him and read, "I MAY HAVE NO WORTH TO YOU, BUT I HAVE WORTH TO GOD."

"God," Billy nodded.

He played soldier as he marched around, head and sign held high. Carolyn and other pro-life volunteers marched with him, handing out pamphlets, and talking with girls and women before they went in, trying with all their might to talk them out of what they planned to do.

Most of the women ignored them, walking past as though they did not exist. A few accepted the literature. For a brief moment, Carolyn had hope. As the women walked away, they dropped it on the ground, without even looking.

Most of the teens dropped their heads, hiding their faces. Some giggled with friends as they filed past.

Carolyn's heart broke as she watched the women and girls go in the brick building, full of life, only to come out empty and bleeding. She imagined each child's life, each baby, holding them, rocking and singing to them. And no one ever would. She thought of each woman as carrying the baby she could have if the woman would let her adopt it. And so she mourned for each one as though it were her own potential child.

She marched, she sang, she prayed, she cried, she pleaded. "Please don't kill your baby. Save a life today. Think again." And no one listened.

By the end of the day, all her emotions and grief had been poured out on the sidewalk in front of the small building she called an abortion mill. She flopped into the car, limp as a rag doll.

The drive home took forever. Her mind could not concentrate on the winding road, but remembered instead the children who would never be.

She looked at sleeping Billy, his pudgy cheek resting on a dirty hand, a tiny stream of drool dripping down his arm. *He does look all of three years old when he sleeps*, Carolyn thought. She put one hand on his leg, hoping to give and receive love through the touch.

Billy came to life as the Camaro bumped up the driveway. He bounced up and down on the seat. "Sissy's house, Sissy's house."

Carolyn moved out of habit, without thought or plan. She sat on her couch, surrounded by fresh flowers, perfect order and designed beauty, sick inside over the ugliness she saw in Morristown.

"Rob, nothing I do ever changes these people. They are determined to abort, no matter what the facts are."

Rob sat next to her, holding her hand, while Billy zoomed around the house as a fighter jet.

"Maybe they don't know what the facts are," he said.

"Oh, they know. How can they ignore our signs, our slogans, our pamphlets? We march to tell them, and still they don't listen."

"Maybe when they come to the clinic, they are at the peak of stress and fear. People can't listen when they're afraid. I think they'd be more able to listen before they get pregnant, or before they get to the clinic."

"How, Rob? How do I reach them before? How can I tell them the facts? How can we save these babies?"

"I don't know. You have always thought of ways to handle all the other causes you've been involved in, I'm sure you'll figure something out this time."

"Do you think I'll make a difference? Do you think all this work will ever change anything?"

"If *you* are involved, things have to change."

Carolyn gave him a feeble smile. "Thanks for your confidence. I only wish I had the same."

"You will tomorrow."

Carolyn cocked her head, confused. "Tomorrow?"

"Saturdays you are always depressed. Come Sunday, everything will be bright again."

She did feel better on Sunday. "Rob, I've realized the problem, and the solution," she said as she zipped her dress for church.

"What's that?"

"I've simply got to push harder. Be louder, more visible. I'll write more letters, put on seminars, bring in movies. Rob, this abortion has got to stop!"

Billy looked frightened. "Sissy mad?"

Carolyn bent down to hug him. "Sissy's not mad at you, Billy. Sissy's mad at the bad ladies."

Billy hugged her back. "Bad ladies. Sissy'll stop 'em." He smiled and strutted off.

Carolyn and Rob laughed. She said to him, "Rob, he's too precious. The thought of him not being here because of someone's whim hurts terribly."

In church, Carolyn could not pay attention to the service. Rob had to jab her twice to remind her to stand up for the hymn. During the sermon her pen flew over the back of the bulletin, writing ideas and plans.

Billy squirmed in his seat, tired of coloring. His arms raised and began to flap. "If I were a bird."

Carolyn automatically reached out to hold one arm down. She dug in her purse for a box of tiny mints, shaking two into Billy's eager hand. "Bird seed for quiet birds," she whispered, then went back to her writing.

* * *

Carolyn and Rob mingled with friends following the service. Within ten minutes, Carolyn had invited five couples and one single parent over for dinner on different nights. Spotting Joann in the crowd, she caught her eye and waved. Joann waved back, motioning for Carolyn to come over.

Carolyn grabbed Billy's hand, and took him to see her.

Joann held out her hand to shake his. "Remember me, Billy? I'm Joann."

Billy looked at Carolyn for approval. "Joann?"

Carolyn nodded. "Joann's a good friend of mine. She bought you a stuffed dog when you were a baby."

Billy smiled as if he remembered. "Joann bought Billy a dog."

"How was Mendocino?" Carolyn asked Joann.

"Beautiful. One of the best dates David and I have been on in a while. How was your movie?" Joann hated to ask. "Was there a good turnout?"

"Excellent. The place was packed. I wish you could have seen it, Joann. You would not have left there unconvinced."

"I'm sure."

Billy skipped away to the stained-glass window, touching and studying it. Carolyn watched him with one eye. "Joann, time is so short. I wish you'd help." Tears welled up in her eyes. "I can't stand to see all those babies lost."

Joann chewed on the inside of her cheek. "Teresa's coming."

Carolyn wiped the tears away. "Good. I want her to meet Billy."

Carolyn thought how pretty Teresa looked, with her long black hair underneath a white hat. Her clothes were never quite in fashion, or matching, but she never looked frumpy or careless, even in jeans and head scarf.

"Teresa, I want you to meet Billy," she said as she went to the window and pulled on Billy's hand.

"Hey, give me five, Billy! I heard you can sing 'Take Me Out to the Ball Game.' "

Billy smiled. "Yep."

"Will you sing it for me?"

The church echoed with the lusty, enthusiastic voice.

"That's the best I ever heard," she told him when he finished.

Billy glowed with pride. "I can sing 'Trust and Obey,' too," he said.

"Then sing it!" Terresa encouraged.

When it was time to go, Billy zipped through the church pews, zigzagging through each row. When he got to the end, he shouted, "Teresa's my friend, Sissy!"

·10·

·· Pulling into the Morristown K-Mart parking lot, Joann spoke. "I've waited two weeks to get this stuff. I hope they have it."

Teresa smiled. "They should."

"So should somebody in River Edge, but they don't."

Teresa pointed toward the front of the store. "Tell me it's not."

"Tell you it's not what?" Joann asked as she looked in the direction Teresa pointed. Carolyn stood there, nodding, gesturing, then pointing at Billy. A couple took the clipboard, taking turns signing.

"I don't believe it," Teresa said. Billy hopped from horse to horse on the coin-operated merry-go-round. "What is she doing?"

Joann turned the car to go back out of the lot. "She's using Billy to get people to sign her antiabortion petition. We'll come back later. I can't stand to see her do that."

"Then why don't you say something?"

Joann looked at her, then shrugged her shoulders. "I don't know. I'm too embarrassed. Besides, anything I say to her, she gets mad about."

"I'll tell her then."

"Good. You can do it later."

"No, now."

"Teresa, I don't want to get into this now. I wanted a nice, relaxing day."

"*Now.* Go back in. Just drive up to her."

The window rolled down as the car pulled up next to Carolyn, the August heat blasting into the air-conditioned car. "I thought that was you, Joann," Carolyn said. "But I couldn't figure out why you were driving in circles."

"We couldn't decide if we should stop or not," Joann said truthfully.

Teresa couldn't wait for the chitchat to end. "Why are you doing this, Carolyn?"

"The petition? It's to get the decision repealed . . ."

"No, why do you have Billy here with you?"

"He's good for business. More people sign when I have living proof. That's why I want Joann to be out here with me. It's a real boost to have a pregnant woman."

"You're exploiting Billy."

"Oh, come on, Teresa. Anything is fair when lives are at stake."

"It's not fair to Billy."

"He doesn't know. He plays and gets an ice cream. That's all he cares about when we're at home, too. This way he's doing something worthwhile. Why don't you two stay and help?"

"I can't believe you, Carolyn. We'll see you later," Teresa said.

Joann took her cue and drove off.

Teresa looked out the window. "How long is Billy staying with Carolyn?"

"Another couple of weeks, I think."

"Let's kidnap him for a day and let that poor kid have some fun."

"Okay. I'm teaching at vacation Bible school next week, but the week after, I'm free. I'll ask Carolyn."

"Do you think she'll part with him for a moment?"

"Who knows."

They spent the rest of the day forgetting about Carolyn and Billy, shopping and laughing, each forgetting something different. Teresa forgot her anger, Joann forgot her guilt.

* * *

Vacation Bible school kept Joann busy for the next week, giving her a convenient excuse to avoid Carolyn. Her anger needed to cool, and her thoughts to be caught together in careful bundles, before she could present one of them to Carolyn.

She taught the six-year-olds, the age her child would have been. And so she loved each child as if it were her own. Sometimes she forgot they weren't hers. She saw Ross in some of them, herself in others. She marveled at their imaginations and their creative abilities. She praised their crafts as if it were the craft her own child had produced. And they loved her.

Each day Joann went home exhilarated and exhausted with a tinge of something heavy around her heart. She always carried the same feeling with her, but this week it was sharper and more noticeable. She never knew what caused the feeling, she only knew it never left. When the week ended, she cried over a loss she couldn't understand.

When Joann saw Carolyn the following Monday, she still bathed in the mellow feeling of satisfaction.

"I went to San Francisco yesterday for a rally," Carolyn said. "I made a point of going to that little fabric store off Union Square and got you something for the baby."

"Again? Carolyn, you've got to stop giving me all this stuff. I'll be sewing for the next hundred years."

"I only do it because I love watching what you create. I wish I had your skill."

"Thanks. How much longer will Billy be with you?" Joann asked.

"Another week."

"Can Teresa and I have him for one day?"

Carolyn's brows pulled together, the smile leaving her face. "Why?"

"We want to get to know him a little better," Joann lied. "You are so busy, we knew we'd never get the four of us together."

"I don't know if I can spare him."

Joann looked away, as if to watch the ski boat going past on the lake. "Just one day?"

"All right. Just one day."

That evening Joann dug through fabric boxes and bags, finding pieces to create a quilt with the new lace panel Carolyn had bought her. In the center of the panel, a bear rode a carousel horse. As she searched for what she needed, she began to reminisce about her friendship with Carolyn.

They had met in junior high, two scared kids, running from class to class, arms piled high with books, because they knew they would never have time to get to their lockers and back to class before the tardy bell rang. Carolyn was tall for a seventh-grader, and Joann, short. Their Phys. Ed. teacher assigned them gym lockers right next to each other, and both girls were so modest they wouldn't look at each other.

They might never have met that year, except one day, as they dressed back to back, Joann reached in the locker for her shorts. When she put them on, she realized they were not hers at all. She turned around to see Carolyn frantically searching for her shorts. Joann turned beet red. "I think I've got your shorts by mistake," she mumbled.

"My shorts?" Carolyn started to say. She took one look at Joann, the shorts around her knees, and broke into hysterics. Joann joined in, and they became best friends forever after that.

Their instant friendship built to one that would last through rival club memberships, boyfriends, dates, slumber parties, and different churches. They lost contact in college, with only a rare note to keep in touch. Then Carolyn had encouraged Joann to move north, out of longing for a friend to share in her life.

Now Joann wanted to repay some of the generous friendship Carolyn had poured out over the years; the shoulder to cry on, the listening ear and understanding heart. The forgiveness when they disagreed, the acceptance when she did something dumb.

Each stitch, as Joann began the piece, reminded her of another kindness, another prayer, another strength Carolyn had given. Few people in this world were lucky enough to have a friendship like she had with Carolyn. She hated the way they disagreed now. Only Joann's defensiveness separated them. Maybe if she told Carolyn why she felt as she did, Carolyn would understand and stop hounding her. *It's over and done with, and doesn't matter anymore. She doesn't need to know.*

·11·

"·· The quality of life," echoed inside Teresa's head as she watched Billy play. He sloshed through the water at the lake's edge, splashing the other children. Their shrieks encouraged him to slosh harder. He smiled with impish glee at each shriek. When he tired of that, Joann towed him around in a plastic ring.

Teresa sat in the sand, her knees pulled up to her chin, a purple visor pulled down over her forehead. *Who says Down's children don't have quality of life?* she thought. *Billy has more life than most anyone else I've met. And quality? Who decides what quality is?*

Billy kicked and flailed, showering Joann until she looked like a drowned rat. Teresa laughed until she cried. When she started crying, she couldn't stop, her tears turning from hilarity to sadness. She hated opening old wounds, of crying over them again and again. *Why can't I leave the past alone? If only I hadn't been so stupid, so naive.* She reached for a towel to wipe the tears and sweat from her face.

Joann sat beside her. "I don't think it's fair to make the pregnant lady play tugboat with a ten-year-old kid."

"You insisted you needed the exercise," Teresa retorted. "Besides, you look the part."

"You'd better behave, or I'll sic Billy on you. You'll have a shower like you've never known."

"Oh, no you won't. Not if you want lunch."

"Of course I want lunch." Joann rubbed her tummy. "This kid eats a lot."

Teresa gulped and looked away. She tried not to think about personalizing it all. That a baby grew inside there. It made her heart hurt, and her eyes swell with tears. *Stupid tears.*

"I'll get lunch ready for us then. I'm hungry too, and Billy must be famished. He's used up more energy than I could in a week of aerobics."

Joann went to the shore to wrap Billy in a towel. Teresa set out plates and sandwiches, pouring cranapple juice into paper cups with spaceships on them.

Billy flapped up to the table, sitting on a bench. "Oh, boy, spaceships!" he shouted, grabbing a cup and pouring the juice down his throat. "Can I have more?"

He peered cautiously inside the sandwich, sticking his finger inside the goo.

"It's peanut butter and honey," Teresa told him. "Do you like that?"

"Sandchip," he said.

"Yes, it's a sandwich."

"Sandchip."

Teresa looked at Joann, who shrugged her shoulders. Teresa reached in the picnic basket and pulled out a cookie can, then reached in again and pulled out a bag of chips. Billy clapped his hands. "Sandchip! Can I have some?"

Teresa doled out a handful of chips. Billy took one and shoved it inside his sandwich. He stopped, and looked at Teresa as if to get her approval. "Go ahead, Billy."

A huge grin crossed his face, his eyes squinting. He took every chip except one and stuffed them all inside the sandwich. "Sandchip," he said, and bit off a corner. After three bites, he jumped down from the bench and did a little dance as he ate.

Teresa poured the cranapple again. "Here, jumping jack. Here's some more juice."

When he finished, Joann gave him three chocolate-chip cookies.
"Joann, Carolyn is not going to be happy with you," Teresa told her.
"If she can give him ice cream every day, I can give him a cookie."
"Three?"
"Every kid needs junk food to grow on."
Billy dashed off to the swings. He called out, "Push me!"
Teresa smiled. "This is my forte." She ran over to Billy, and gave him a shove. He began to pump, still calling, "Push me!"
At four o'clock, they peeled Billy away from the slide, and put him and the picnic basket in the car. He fell asleep before they hit the street, not waking up until they pulled into Carolyn's driveway. "Sissy's house!"
Carolyn met them at the door. "Hi, Billy. Did you have a good day?"
"Sissy! I swam, I swinged, I got to tickle Joann's baby in there. My feet were cold and soft, I even had a sandchip!"
Teresa pulled off her visor. "We had a wonderful day. Scorching, but wonderful."
Joann tousled Billy's hair. "He's crazy, Carolyn."
Carolyn looked angry, Joann confused.
Teresa was disgusted. "Carolyn, she didn't mean it literally. It's only an expression. Don't be so sensitive."
Joann flushed. "Carolyn. I wasn't thinking. I'm sorry."
Carolyn's lips were drawn in a tight line. "I'm glad you had a good day. I'd better get Billy bathed and ready for dinner and bed. See you on Sunday?"
They both nodded.

✳   ✳   ✳

Quality of life. Quality of life. Quality of life, chanted the soldiers marching through Teresa's head that night as she tried to go to sleep. She slipped out of bed without waking Dan. She knelt by the couch, her head down on her arms, slow tears soaking everything. "God," she whispered. "I'm so sorry. I never would have done it if I had known. And so much is gone now. It would have happened anyway, I couldn't have stopped it, but why did I have to be a part of it? Oh God. Forgive me again."
She crept back in bed. As peace washed over her, she fell asleep.
The next morning, Teresa gave Dan a long good-bye kiss and tucked a prayer list into his pocket before sending him and his lunch off to work. She knew Dan prayed, and he got answers. They weren't the type of prayers many people wanted him to pray. They asked for physical

healing; he prayed for emotional healing, strength, and peace. They asked God to change the situation. He asked God to change the person, and give out large dollops of wisdom. Today he would pray her job interview would go well, even if she didn't get the job.

She thanked God for her peaceful relationship with Dan. It gave her one less thing to worry about. She couldn't have dealt with the stress of a troubled relationship as well as her own troubled heart. Dan helped her to heal, to wear her mask well so others need not be burdened with her burdens. One day, the right time would come for her to use the pain to heal another, but not yet.

She dressed, choosing clothes that reflected what she wanted to express—casual yet conservative, comfortable with herself. The fawn-colored dress looked horrible on most people, but on her, it set off her brown eyes and dark hair to bring out her Native American heritage.

The dentist's office sat on the edge of the lake. She opened the door, was greeted by an efficient receptionist, and handed an application to fill out.

After returning the completed application to the receptionist, Teresa wanted to pace the floor. Instead she picked up a magazine, flipping through it, trying to be aware of her crossed foot, and not letting it bounce too much. She hated being nervous.

"Teresa Meyer," the receptionist called from the opened door.

Teresa smiled at her, following her into the office where the dentist sat behind his desk, surrounded by walls of degrees and certificates stating what school, what year, what honor, what purpose for each piece of paper.

A small man, Dr. Willer had big, toothy grin. "Hello, Teresa," he said, offering his hand. Teresa smiled back, shaking his hand with a firm grip.

"I see from your experience that you have never worked in a dental office before. Why did you decide to change from being a physician's assistant to a dental assistant?"

Teresa swallowed before answering. "I felt a change, a diversity from what I am used to would be a challenge to me," she said, hoping her response didn't sound as canned as it was.

"Do you realize this job has entirely different responsibilities?"

"Yes, sir, I do."

"What about training?"

"Your receptionist said you would be willing to train. I learn quickly, and could spend my evenings reading any manuals or other helpful materials you could give me."

The interview concluded with a tour of the treatment rooms and lab. Teresa sensed Dr. Willer's pride over his domain. The treatment rooms had sliding glass doors that led outside to the lakeshore. Mount Sakar could be seen across the lake. "These rooms are beautiful," Teresa remarked. "Much better than staring at a blank wall, or even a poster."

"We find our patients more relaxed in this atmosphere. Their experience in the dental office is a good one. We try to make sure of that. Here we have earphones and a radio so they can listen to their favorite music. I have found, with the earphones on, they cannot hear the drill as well. This also helps them relax."

Teresa enjoyed hearing this man speak with concern for his patients. The last physician she worked for spoke of the same concerns, but his actions didn't coincide with his words. She detected sincerity in Dr. Willer. She knew Dan prayed right now for her, that she'd know whether to accept if offered the job. She didn't want to live with the same confusion and frustrations as before.

Dr. Willer shook her hand, promising to call her in a week with an answer. He had more interviews, with some more qualified than she. Teresa walked to her car in the warm sunshine, confident that she had done her best, no matter what the outcome.

* * *

Two weeks later, Teresa turned in front of the mirror, checking out her new uniform. Comfortable white nurse's shoes stuck their ugly noses out from underneath her pants. Dan came up behind her, putting his arms around her waist, his chin on her shoulder. "Scared?"

"Yes, and excited. I finished all the workbooks, so now it's on-the-job training."

"I knew you'd get the job."

"I didn't. I never thought I'd have a chance with experienced applicants."

"Your sweet smile won him over."

"I bet it was my answer to his last question."

"What was that?"

"He had shown me all the instruments and where they belonged. I thought it odd for him to do that with someone who didn't have the job yet. Then at the very end, he said, 'Where is the explorer?' I told him which drawer it was in, as well as telling him where I saw one that seemed to be misplaced. His smile told me I had said the right thing. It must have been a test."

"You bet. You know, I prayed he would notice your awareness of things around you. I think you really need it in this kind of job."

"It was a big detriment in my last job."

"I know. Don't think about that. Think about your new job, and the new possibilities you have here." He kissed her cheek, and she turned to kiss him full and long on the mouth. "How is a man supposed to go to work with a send-off like that?" he asked her.

Teresa shrugged her shoulders and smiled. "With a smile on his face?"

He patted her behind, picked up his lunch and the church bulletin prayer insert. "Bye, T. See you when I deliver the mail!"

* * *

Teresa loved her job, learning quickly, as she promised. She tried, but didn't get, Tuesday mornings off to go to Bible study. She did have an hour and a half lunch, which she took either in the park, with Dan, or with Joann and sometimes with Carolyn if she could ever get her snagged between commitments. On rare occasions, she'd get both Joann and Carolyn together. Those times could be interesting, silly, or explosive, depending on the conversation. Teresa tried to troubleshoot and control the direction of the conversation, hoping to avoid confrontation between Carolyn and Joann. One day it would come to a head, threatening their friendship, she knew. She only hoped they would be strong enough to pick up the pieces.

·12·

••**I** only come over here because you have air conditioning, you know," Vicki said to Joann as she entered the cool apartment.

"I think I'd die if I didn't have it. How hot is it today, anyway?"

"The bank says a hundred and ten degrees."

"Really? Do you think it's right?"

"It usually is. Last summer we had six days in a row of a hundred and twelve."

Joann shook her head. "I thought we were crazy to choose one apartment over another simply because it had air conditioning. Now I'm glad we did."

"Me, too. Look what I did last night."

Joann peered into a box of black things. "Brownies?"

"Yeah. They are a little heavy, but I thought you might like them."

Joann tried to take a bite. "A *little* heavy?"

"C'mon. Betty Crocker, I'm not."

They pulled out their needlework, and Joann gave her little lesson for the day. As they worked, they talked.

"Joann, you'll never guess what happened to me yesterday."

"When you went to the barbecue at the lake?"

"Yeah. I met this gorgeous guy."

Joann rolled her eyes. "Yet another perfect man for the Vick."

"Now, wait a minute. This guy is truly a god. Tall, blond, works out with weights, so you can imagine what his body looks like without a shirt."

"Did you have to imagine?"

"Heavens, no. He left very little to the imagination. Anyway, I thought there was no way he'd look at me."

"So what did you do?"

"I went down the hot slide and burned my behind."

"Oh, Vicki, you didn't."

"Well, I took a little kid with me who was scared to go alone."

"I'll bet."

"I only had to pay him a quarter to pretend he was scared."

"Oh, Vicki!"

"It worked. Ol' handsome took notice. He says he loves long hair."

"So then what?"

"We talked all afternoon. Swam some too. His folks own a ski boat, so I can go skiing with him soon. Nice to kill two birds with one stone. Not only do I hook a winner, but he has a ski boat to top it off."

"I'm surprised you didn't find that out first."

"Well, I sort of asked questions, but I really wasn't going to make up my mind based on the answer. Ouch!" She stuck her bleeding finger into her mouth.

"Slow down. Your work gets sloppy when you talk about guys."

"Can't help it. I've got a one-track mind."

"What's his name, anyway?"

"Martin."

"Martin? No one has a name like Martin."

"You do if you have a lot of money and you are Martin Fleming *Salinger* the third."

"Money? Mr. Right? Vicki, aren't you ashamed?"

"Of course not. I'll marry for money. I'm not proud."

Joann dropped her work. "Vicki, don't you think there's more to life than money?"

"Sure, but what?" Vicki paused for drama's sake. "Just kidding, Joann. I really do think he's nice. There's something appealing about how much he cares for his body and takes care of it. I could probably learn something from him."

"I'm not commenting on that one!"

Vicki laughed. "We both know I could use some help in caring for this body. I never thought it mattered."

* * *

"My two hours are up," Vicki said, cramming her stuff into a bag. "You can stay if you want."

"No, I can't. I have to be home if I want Mom to be civil to me. It's dinner at six or pay the consequences for the rest of the night for being late."

Joann hated how casually Vicki talked of her horrible life at home. Joann wanted to change it all, but didn't know what to do. She invited Vicki over as much as possible, and took her to her OB appointments, shopping, whatever she could do to occupy Vicki rather than for her to be at home, or hanging out at the park. It didn't seem like much, but it was all she could think of.

As Vicki hopped on her bike, Joann stopped her. "I almost forgot. Would you like to go with Carolyn, Teresa, and me to the City a week from Saturday? We're going to shop and have some fun."

"Can we ride the cable cars?"

"Of course."

"I'll come."

"We'll be home late."

"I think since you're going, and it's a special thing, that will be okay."

83

·13·

·· Vicki couldn't sit still. The closer they got to San Francisco the more she squirmed and bounced. "Who invited her?" Carolyn teased.

"I confess," Joann said. "I thought she needed time away from her cage."

Everyone laughed. Teresa said, "Looks like you were right. I never knew you had such intuition, Joann."

"Whoa!" exclaimed Carolyn. "Let me tell you about this woman's intuition! In high school, she always knew what teacher of hers would pop a quiz and when. She knew who would ask who out and when someone was about ready to drop someone else. This woman is spooky."

"Oh, good," Vicki said. "Maybe you can tell me if Martin is the man for me."

"Who's Martin?" Teresa asked.

"Only the cutest guy that ever walked this earth."

"When do we get to meet him?" Carolyn asked.

"Walk by the theater Monday night about ten to seven. We will be buying tickets."

"A real date?" Joann asked. "When did this happen?"

"Last night. He wanted me to go out with him tonight."

"And you turned him down for us?"

"Well, not for you, for the City. I will turn anyone down at a chance to go to San Francisco for the day."

"I'm glad you came," Teresa said. "I hear everyone talk about you, but I never have gotten a chance to. Tell me more about yourself."

"What's there to say? I'm sixteen, lazy, a klutz, and in love with a gorgeous *rich* guy. My parents drink to drown some sorrow they've never told me about. My brother is in and out of jail for one thing or another."

"You think a lot of yourself, don't you?" Teresa said sarcastically.

"Oh, those are the good points. I won't tell anyone the bad."

Joann spoke up. "Vicki has a wonderful sense of humor, will listen to me complain for hours. Is willing to struggle to learn new things. She is cute and brightens anyone's day."

"What Vicki are you talking about?" Vicki asked, trying to cover her embarrassment.

"Silly goose," Joann said. "You're a special person and you don't even know it."

"Agreed," Teresa said.

"I think so too," Carolyn said in her tone no one could question.

The Golden Gate Bridge spanned the waters, glinting in the sun. "No fog, we're lucky today," said Carolyn.

Teresa pointed to the ocean side. "It's hovering off over there like a monster waiting to devour the City."

"It does, too," replied Carolyn.

Joann loved the City. This would be her third trip. She never drove, and refused to. The maniacal drivers turned the traffic into chaos. One had to be ruthless to battle for position with the cable cars, taxis, delivery trucks, and buses. Pedestrians ignored the signals and crosswalks. A parking place did not exist unless you knew your way around to find a spot on an obscure street. Joann didn't think she needed to have a heart attack at the ripe old age of twenty-six.

Carolyn, on the other hand, drove like a resident. She seemed more at home in the City than in Lake Ridge. She knew all the secrets and loved to share them with friends.

"Where to first?" she called over her shoulder.

"How about a tour of the park," requested Teresa.

"Objections?"

"None," replied Joann and Vicki.

The park had more of a traffic jam than the rest of the city. Bikers, runners, walkers, picnickers all used the streets with casual aplomb. Drivers searched for parking spots, another hopeless chase.

Vicki leaned out her window. "Hey, cutie. Can we get together sometime?"

Joann yanked her back inside. "Vicki, what are you doing?"

"Didn't you see how cute that guy was?"

"I don't care how cute he was. Don't yell at him."

Teresa laughed. "Didn't you ever do that when you were in high school?"

Carolyn shook her head. "Not Joann. She was too shy."

"I sure wanted to, though," Joann added.

"I'll do it for both of us, then," Vicki offered, then stuck her head out the window again, waving and shouting at a group of high-school boys walking by wearing shorts, their T-shirts tied around their waists, and tennis shoes with no socks. One carried a Frisbee. "Can I play too?" Vicki called.

"Anytime, sweetheart," called back the tallest one.

Joann yanked her back in again. "C'mon, I don't need a bunch of high-school guys chasing after us."

"They'd never do that," Vicki insisted.

"With all that come on, of course they would," Carolyn said.

Teresa waved a hand at them all. "I'm with Vicki. I don't see any harm in flirting. But, Vicki, maybe for us old fuddy-duddies, you ought to do without the flirting this trip."

After the park, they drove through streets lined with Victorian homes, forty-year-old apartments that had huge common entry doors with marble steps leading up to them, and, visible through the glass doors, red carpet leading down the hall.

They oohed and aahed properly for their tour guide, who managed to guide as well as drive. Joann thought she'd lose her stomach on some of the steep hills as they dropped straight down. The worst was the crooked Lombard street.

Carolyn found a parking place not too far from Union Square. Vicki skipped her way through sleeping bums without seeming to see them.

"How can she do that?" asked Carolyn, pulling her sweater around her, so it wouldn't touch something it shouldn't, even by accident. "I feel dirty just walking through. She acts like it's a field of daisies."

Teresa looked at Carolyn, shocked at her attitude. "I thought you loved to help the person down on his luck."

"Down on his luck maybe, but not just plain lazy."

"Who said they're lazy?"

"Well, aren't they? Isn't there work to be looked for? to be had? Why spend your life drinking and sleeping and panhandling?"

Joann looked at them, wishing she had money to feed and clothe them all. "I bet that some of them have tried. They lost their families, their jobs, their self-esteem. After a long time of trying, of praying, and getting no answers, people just give up."

Teresa shook her head. "You know, neither of you makes sense to me. Joann has all the compassion and understanding in the world for these bums on the benches, but will say nothing public against abortion. And Carolyn holds rallies about the importance of each human life, and cringes when she sees some of the life gone wrong. I think Vicki has better sense sometimes than either of you. When are you going to even out?" She stepped up her pace, to catch up with Vicki.

Joann and Carolyn looked at each other in self-righteous confusion. "I've never heard Teresa get mad at anybody for anything," Carolyn said.

"Except when she saw you getting signatures with Billy."

"Do you think she's right?"

"Sometimes. Maybe she doesn't understand God has given us all different compassions."

"Do you really think so?" asked Carolyn, still clutching her sweater and purse against her body. "Or do you think we should all have like compassions?"

"I don't think we can all do everything. I think God gives us a corner to work on, and we'd better put our all into that corner."

"I still think God put you in my corner," Carolyn said.

"I don't. Look, the signal's changing. Let's hurry to catch it."

Joann had never seen a store like Macy's—eight stories of hustle and bustle of high fashion. Stools scattered about the vast cosmetics department were perched on by women being painted and told how they could look their best.

No one bought anything except Carolyn, who bought a silk blouse and paid more for it than Joann had for her last two dresses.

Joann didn't want to cross the street to visit the children's department. She knew she would only long for the beautiful things she could never afford. But the rest of the group wouldn't dream of leaving without checking out the infant dresses and accessories.

"Isn't this adorable?" Teresa held a tiny dotted swiss dress with a frilly lace petticoat attached.

"It's so tiny!" Vicki exclaimed.

Carolyn examined each dress with the intensity of a mother choosing the perfect dress for her child's dedication. Then she wandered over to the boys' rack and examined each tiny suit in the same way.

Joann's heart melted over so many of the items. Some clothes, for some unexplained reason, brought tears to her eyes. She felt stupid and wiped them away before anyone noticed.

"Look at this, can you believe it?" Vicki called, holding up a tiny pair of cowboy boots in one hand, and tiny pink Nikes in the other. "Which will it be, Joann, the boots or the Nikes?"

"Either, I only want a baby."

"What's your favorite?" Carolyn asked Joann.

"My favorite what?"

"Choose two outfits, one for a boy, the other for a girl. As soon as I know what you have, I'll come get it for you."

"No, silly. You can't spend that much money."

"You watch. Now choose."

"I couldn't."

Teresa stepped up holding a yellow dress. Two rosebud ribbons were pinned to the bodice. Layers of ruffles flowed down from them in tiers, each tier with a row of lace around it. "I watched her look at this one the longest. I bet she even cried, but wouldn't admit it now."

Joann looked to the ground, embarrassed. She did love that dress, and had imagined what her child would look like in it.

Vicki raced over with a blue combed-cotton suit. On a separate hanger hung a light blue shirt, with a tiny tie clasped to the collar. "I vote for this one, Joann. Like it?"

"Sure, it's adorable. But I can't have Carolyn spending money on me like this."

Teresa put her hand on Joann's arm. "I think it makes her feel good, and not so cheated about not being able to buy nice things for her own baby."

Carolyn looked grateful. "A person has to let her best friend know how much she is loved."

"Thanks, Carolyn. But don't feel obligated. I won't expect it."

"Good. It will be a surprise then."

At one o'clock Carolyn led them up a tiny side street to an ugly old building. Inside, they boarded a rickety, open elevator. It groaned up to the third floor, and opened its gate into a quaint cafe. The ring of silverware touching fine china made a delicate sound in the air. A cage of finches sang little melodies to serenade the guests. The hostess seated them at a linen-covered table, set with crystal and china. "Real silver?" Vicki asked, a little too loudly.

The menu was hand painted with scrolled flowers, the choices done in calligraphy. Roses decorated one menu, another violets, another silver bells, and Vicki's had tiny birds.

The meal matched the delicacy and elegance of the atmosphere. The waiter placed a large bowl of fresh-cut fruit in the center of the table. Each lady had her own plate, serving herself from the common bowl in the center.

When they finished the fruit, the waiter set steaming chicken crepes in front of them with baby vegetables on the side. A bowl of sherbet finished off the meal.

Carolyn picked up the bill, waving away their attempts to pay for their own portion. "This is my treat. I brought you here, knowing you would have probably chosen Burger King."

Vicki nodded. "That would have been my vote, but I'm glad I was overruled."

"Carolyn, you are too generous," Joann pleaded.

"One can never be too generous."

"Thank you very much. I haven't felt so nice in a long time," Teresa said.

"Thank you, Carolyn," Joann said, "it really was nice. I've never felt so exquisite and pampered."

The group walked to the north side of Union Square to catch the cable car to the Wharf. Vicki and Teresa stood on the outside of the car holding the poles, shrieking with delight whenever the car turned a sharp corner. Joann and Carolyn sat facing them, content with the safety of their seats.

Joann smiled at Vicki's exuberance. Vicki had become a friend, a little sister. They had talked about Vicki's home, her dreams, and about school. Vicki didn't seem to have a serious side. She described life as fun and games with no pain, no terror, no sadness—only laughter and sunshine.

Joann worried about Vicki's lack of goals and friends. She worried about Vicki's naive obsession with boys.

The Wharf appeared too soon. After browsing around Ghiradelli Square and checking out the street artisans, they hailed two pedicabs. They rode in style to Pier 39, a busy tourist trap. They teased the pedicab drivers all the way to the pier, Vicki calling out to pedestrians as if they were old friends.

The pier jostled more people than Macy's ever thought of putting through her doors, except maybe during the Christmas season. Sweaty horses trotted by, pulling buggies with lovers and old ladies. The arcade rang, buzzed, twittered, and banged as people dropped quarters to test their skills.

The stores along the pier sported novelty items, each overpriced for the tourist. Teresa bought some anyway. Joann succumbed to temptation in the Christmas store, buying one ornament for her tree. She loved bears, and this one, peeking over a manger at the baby Jesus, proved too much for her to pass.

A two-story Victorian carousel spun in musical circles, beckoning to the kid in each of them. They gave in, enjoying the memories that played in each mind. Imaginations of riding in the Old West, for Teresa; a princess riding her steed about the castle grounds, for Vicki; while Carolyn had ridden her thoroughbred to victory in the Kentucky Derby. Joann smiled, remembering her fantasies of owning her own horse that all her friends could ride, making her enemies jealous.

They left their memories behind for a loaf of sourdough bread and a cup of crab or shrimp cocktail. Vicki berated the merchants for dropping live shellfish into the vats of smelly, boiling water. She threatened two of them with turning them in to the humane society before turning away to laugh. She danced with the street performers and begged an animal balloon from a clown.

Joann thought her feet would drop off before she reached the cable car turnaround, her belly heavy and strained with the baby weight inside. She longed to have Vicki's energy, which didn't seem to diminish any during the day.

The jerky ride back to Union Square on the cable car hurt each inch of Joann's tired body. The baby woke up. "I think it's doing aerobics already," she told Carolyn.

"Good," Carolyn yawned. "It's already smarter than its mother."

·14·

··Teresa offered to drive home, and Carolyn accepted. Joann fell asleep after the car crossed the Golden Gate Bridge. Carolyn fell asleep about twenty miles after Joann.

Vicki rolled down her window, sticking her face into the warm breeze.

"Did you have fun today, Vicki?" Teresa asked.

"Oh, you bet. Did you?"

"Yes, I did. I don't think I've had such a good day in a long time."

The wind pushed Vicki's arm backwards as she stuck it out the window. "I'm glad you guys let me tag along. I know I can be a pest sometimes."

"You weren't a pest today. I enjoyed your company."

Vicki looked surprised. "Do you really mean that?"

"I do." Teresa changed lanes, zipping past an ancient truck loaded with broken-down furniture. It pulled an ugly, decrepit pink trailer.

"It's the Beverly Hillbillies!" Vicki said.

Teresa laughed, then her voice got serious. "I wonder if that's all they own, camping from place to place."

Vicki's face drew tight. "What makes you think that?"

Teresa shrugged. "When I was growing up, my family used to camp during the summer. Sometimes we would run into a family camping because they had no other home. My mom always cried when she saw dirty babies, knowing they had no home and probably not enough to eat. She'd leave food with them when we moved on, making it sound like we had no place to store it during a long, hot drive home."

Vicki's right foot began to tap the floor. She looked up at the ceiling, then out the window. Teresa caught a glimpse of her wiping an eye. In a soft voice, she asked, "What's wrong, Vicki?"

Vicki shook her head and swallowed real hard. "We used to live like that. I liked it at first, and then I got tired of not having anything the other kids had. My parents drove me to the nearest school."

"That was nice of them to see you had schooling, even if you didn't have anything else."

"They didn't do it to be nice. They did it to get rid of me for the day, so they wouldn't have to watch out for me."

Vicki looked out the window. Teresa counted three exits before Vicki spoke again. "The kids at school made fun of me. I couldn't take a bath, so I was always dirty and smelled like campfires and sweat. They'd talk about something they saw on TV, and I had no idea what they were talking about. Sometimes Mom and Dad drank so much during the day, they'd forget to pick me up."

Teresa sat, stunned, driving in a daze. Vicki's tears came steadily for a few minutes. Then as abruptly as her emotions opened up, they closed down again. She wiped her cheeks with the bottom of her shirt, then tucked it back in again. She pulled her braid over her shoulder, pulling out the rubber band and unwinding the strands. "That's why I'm happy."

Confused, Teresa figured there must have been some train of thought she had missed.

"Nothing could be worse than not having a home, a place to wash, enough food to eat," Vicki continued. "I prayed every night by that campfire that God would give us a house, any house, and I would be happy. I've kept my promise."

"Don't you think it's okay with God for you to be sad?"

"There's nothing to be sad about anymore." She pulled a black brush through the length of hair until it was smooth. Then she pulled it to one side and braided it. "You won't tell Joann or Carolyn, will you? I never would have told you, but. . . ."

"I won't tell. I think you could tell Joann. She seems to be sad about something too. Maybe you could help her, if she knew how hurt you have been."

"I'm not telling."

"Okay."

"What is your family like, Teresa?"

"My folks taught me to love Jesus, and to help those who hurt. I watched them live what they believed. Dad, kind and gentle, yet strong—in character and body—spent many of his off hours caring for single moms. He'd mow their yards, wash their windows, paint, whatever needed to be done. His buddies laughed at him, certain he must be getting some special payment on the side. He'd smile at them and not even give them the courtesy of an answer."

"And your mom fed vagrants in campgrounds."

"Yes, and fed many strangers Dad brought home. She had a tender heart for the 'fallen' as she called them."

"Who are they?"

"People of the church who woke up to the wrong they were in the middle of. My mom would open her big arms and love them. She never judged them for what they did, and seemed to understand why they did it. Few of them ever made the same mistake after Mom 'loved them back to Jesus.' "

"Do you have any brothers or sisters?"

"I had one brother, but he died before I was born. Mom tried, but couldn't have any more kids."

"It sounds like the perfect family." Vicki sounded disappointed.

Teresa let out half a laugh. "Nothing is ever perfect. When I was a tiny little girl, my dad yelled at Mom a lot. He wasn't satisfied with his work, his life, or himself. He didn't show her any affection. He treated her like a hired servant."

"Do you remember all this?"

"No, only some of the yelling. Mom and Dad told me the whole story when I was a teenager after they heard me telling everyone how perfect they were."

"That's different. So what happened next?"

"My mom had a brief affair. Dad found out and blew up. He threatened to kick her out. For once in her life, she yelled back and told him she was starved for his love. She was sorry for the wrong way she got it, but if he didn't give her love, she'd die."

"Wow."

"Dad listened. From then on, they worked hard at their relationship. I would never trade them for anything."

"I'd trade mine for the next set that came along," Vicki laughed.

Teresa didn't say anything. She couldn't. She couldn't give her the pat answers she heard in church—how God gave you your parents. She knew God could turn evil around for good in people's lives. But they sometimes had to learn that for themselves. To hear good could come of having alcoholic parents who never gave you what you needed sounded too idealistic. The good wouldn't come without lots of hurt, and acceptance of that hurt.

She reached over and touched Vicki's leg. "I'm sorry your life has been so hard. I wish I could help."

Vicki looked out the window and nodded. "Look!" she pointed. "A full moon! And we're missing it rise over Sakar."

"Weirdos come out during full moons."

Vicki turned to look at her, one eyebrow raised. "That's me."

"Oh, Vicki."

Teresa dropped Vicki off first. "See ya later, Vick."

"Yeah. Maybe I'll introduce you to the Hillbillies one day."

"It's a deal."

Carolyn stretched in the backseat. "What are you talking about?"

"It's a joke," Teresa said.

Joann opened her eyes. "Are we home yet?"

Vicki said, "I am, but you aren't. Here, keep my stuff for me, would ya? I don't want my mom to see it. She'd have a cow."

"Joann's having the cow," Teresa teased.

She and Vicki laughed. Carolyn said in a bored tone, "Home, James."

"Bye!"

Teresa turned the car over to Carolyn at the apartments. "Thanks again, Carolyn. The trip was fun, lunch fabulous."

"You're welcome. Next month, we'll go to Napa."

"It's a date."

"We'll do the hot mud baths."

Joann choked. "I'll pass."

They whispered their good-byes, so they wouldn't wake the others in the complex.

Teresa felt shaky after she opened the door. Dan greeted her. She told him about the day, but not about Vicki. Her heart felt sick. It didn't seem fair that some people had a good life and others got the rug pulled out from under them time and time again.

·15·

.. Carolyn stood in front of the post office, distracting people as they went inside to do their business. Her hair stuck to her forehead and neck, as the sun scorched her skin. Her enthusiasm had slipped away. *The situation is hopeless.* The people walking in and out of the post office only cared about their mail. They didn't care about millions dying. They didn't care that their city had lost many important future citizens. They didn't care, and their apathy made her want to scream.

"This is a feminist issue," one well-dressed woman said loudly to Carolyn. "We are not equal with men, and never will be until we have reproductive freedom as they do. This is my body, and nobody will tell me I have to bear children if I don't want to."

Carolyn didn't have energy for a battle against the absurd feminist viewpoint today. She spoke anyway, her voice dripping with sarcasm. "There is something new out. It's called contraception."

"There is also contraceptive failure," the woman retorted.

"Then get your tubes tied. If people were more responsible in sex, there would be fewer unwanted pregnancies."

"Unwanted pregnancies result in unwanted children."

Carolyn sighed. "There are no unwanted children. Do you realize how many women change their minds several months into the pregnancy, or how many couples are waiting for children to adopt?"

"It is an intrusion worse than death to force a woman to allow her body to be distorted, her emotions and her system fouled up for nine months, so someone else can have the product of that distortion."

"Pregnancy is beautiful, it gives life."

"Pregnancy is a parasite, sucking life from the woman."

Carolyn shook, her voice rising to a shriek. "I would give anything for a parasite like that, *anything!*" The firm control broke apart, tears coming in torrents. "And feminists like you distort the whole issue for convenience. *I hate you!*" she screamed.

The woman smiled triumphantly. "And pro-lifers like you preach compassion and never show any. When you can be civil rather than rude, perhaps we can talk." She whirled around, disappearing into the post office.

Carolyn crossed the street to the park, alone, frustrated. She pulled a used tissue from her purse, dabbing at the corners of her eyes, then blowing her runny nose. *Nothing I do is going to make a difference. I try and try. But nobody cares. They only care about themselves, their lives. No intrusions into my life, please. Make it easy for me. Take away the handicaps, the pain, the surprise children. Take away anything that hinders my career, my plans. Oh God, they make me sick. Nobody cares!*

She sat on a huge lawn swing, tucking her knees under her chin. Tears rolled down her cheeks running streaks in her makeup as she tried to cry away the pain. "God," she whispered. "Why do I have to care so much? Why did You burden me with this hopeless task? They can save baby seals, save laboratory animals, and rationalize the slaughter of tiny babies. How sick our nation has become! Animals have more rights than humans. Oh God. It's so sick. I can't take it anymore."

She jumped up. "And you!" she said, pounding her stomach. "You lie there flat and ugly, slack and apathetic about doing your job too!"

She plopped down, and looked at the lake filled with fishermen, skiers, pleasure boaters. She scanned the hills and mountains that rimmed the lake. She never tired of them, even when the merciless sun turned the grass brown. The dark patches of scrub oak mingled with the brown patches, making the hills look like a poodle shaved too close. Sailboats skimmed the water, carefree as she would like to be.

For two more hours she watched, her thoughts tiny tornados in her head, then she got in her Camaro and drove home. At home she opened her front door, cool air greeting her. She threw the clipboard on the kitchen counter with her keys and purse. Opening the refrigerator, she pulled out a Hansen's Apple Lite. It refreshed her throat, but her mind still stewed in frustration and sorrow. She dialed the phone, then sat down at the kitchen table to wait while it rang.

"Hi, Mom. Let me talk to Billy. Yeah, I miss him." She took another long drink before Billy answered.

"Sissy! Hi! I'm playing with my car. Varoom!"

"I'm glad, Billy. I miss you. I wish you were here."

"I had an ice cream, Sissy. Ice cream man gave it to me."

"I'm glad, Billy. You're special to me. I want you to know that, Billy. Do you understand?"

"Yep. Varoom. My car's red, Sissy."

Carolyn hung up, feeling more lonely than before. The quiet house needed children. It needed Billy. She pulled broccoli, carrots, celery, and onions from the refrigerator, slicing them for a Chinese stir-fry dinner.

Rob came in and kissed her on the cheek. "How'd it go today, Carolyn?"

"Awful." She complained of the heat, the apathy, the woman outside the post office.

Rob sat in a kitchen chair, loosening his tie. "Do you ever listen to the other side?"

"Of course I do. It's obnoxious."

"No, I mean really listen."

"I don't need to. . . ."

"Maybe you'd learn something . . . a new approach, a new idea to unravel."

Carolyn slammed the knife down. "I don't need to learn something from them. They are sick. Their approach is sick."

"Maybe there's something you're missing."

"Sure, I'm missing something. More money, more help, more people speaking up for what is right."

"They think they're right, too. So who's right?"

"Whose side are you on, anyway?" Carolyn chopped ferociously.

Rob pushed his thumbs together. "I think you need to examine all the facts. See both sides of the issue before you make dogmatic judgments. Pro-choice believes as strongly in their side as you do in yours. The court sided with them, so there must be some truth to something they are saying. I think you would be wise to hear what they are saying, and examine your own position. Don't be so afraid of finding out you have been wrong in some area."

"I'm not wrong, Rob! Killing babies is wrong."

"I'm not saying it isn't wrong. I'm saying your approach might be wrong, lacking in something. I feel you are dogmatic without knowing the facts."

"What more do I need to know? I know enough." She scooped up the vegetables, dropping them into the hot oil in the wok. Rob came over to her, slipping his arms around her waist. "I love you," he said.

She squirmed away from his grip. "Not now, okay?"

"Are you mad?"

"Yes."

She hated Rob sometimes. She hated his logical, factual mind. He could never rest until he had all sides of every story. Facts, ma'am, give him the facts. *Doesn't he ever feel?* She was sick of the facts. Gory, gross, bloody facts. They swam in her head, making her feel scattered and disjointed.

She couldn't always pull her thoughts together anymore. They fragmented into tiny pieces, as hard to gather as broken glass.

She brooded over dinner, watching each bite go into her mouth as though someone fed her.

Rob scooped the last bite onto his fork before speaking. "I think you need a day off, Carolyn."

"I don't."

"You do. Even Jesus took time alone when the pressure got too much."

Carolyn put bite after tasteless bite into her mouth.

"We're going skiing tomorrow," Rob told her.

"Who?" she asked, her voice flat, uncaring.

"Teresa, Dan, and David."

"What about Joann?"

"She said she's getting too big to be bounced around in a boat all day. She's going to stay home and make us dinner."

Carolyn could feel a tiny smile begin to pull at the corners of her mouth. "Joann? Make dinner? What are we going to have? Mexican TV dinners?"

Rob smiled. "She said she'd barbecue ribs."

"Does she know how?"

"We'll find out, won't we?"

The droning of a ski boat woke Carolyn next morning. She exercised, showered, then fixed her and Rob omelets for breakfast. As she pulled her suit on, she wailed, "Rob, I don't have a tan this year."

"I told you, you've been working too hard."

"And you don't?"

"I know how to relax. You don't believe in the word."

Carolyn took that as a compliment.

Rob knew the owner of Lakeside Boat Rentals. So not only did they get a discount on the rental, but they also got the best boat in the yard.

Carolyn loved to ski. It was the only time she felt free and in complete control. Any other time, she tried to be in control, but couldn't seem to succeed.

The boat roared ahead of her, but she didn't see it. She saw the water, smooth and blue beneath her. She felt the wind, rushing at her face and body, her feet sensitive to the change in texture of the water. Directly behind the boat was like being pulled across a washboard to the side, like butter. Off to the side of the wake, she gathered her freedom. She cut rooster tails, the spray of water shooting away from her.

In ecstasy, her strength flowed, alive, in control. She rarely fell, taking risks, and succeeding. The driver of the boat, the flag holder, both performed at her whim, at her need. She did what she wanted, and she succeeded.

She wished Billy could learn. He would be a bird then, flying through the water. But Billy couldn't swim. His immature coordination kept him paddling in inflatable tubes.

She hated throwing the tow rope in the air, her turn over. Back in the boat, she couldn't come back to reality. She sat in the boat, unfeeling. Not seeing, not hearing; if she kept her eyes closed, the bubble of pleasure could not burst.

"Carolyn. Carolyn." A hand touched her arm. "Come drive for me," Rob said. She nodded in response.

The boat spray showered the riders in a fine mist. Carolyn laughed at Rob's conservative skiing. He couldn't see without his glasses, so his face took on a look of concentration. She shook her head, wondering if he ever did anything with wild abandon. The thought bugged her as she inched the throttle forward, watching Rob bouncing along. She occasionally glanced forward to steer the boat. She watched the furrows on his brow grow deeper, his grip tighter. His body bent over, his arms too far out in front of him. He tried to give her the thumbs-down signal, so she would slow the boat. In the process, he lost balance, tumbling face first into the water.

Carolyn held in her smile as she turned the boat around to bring him the tow rope again. "Carolyn," he sputtered. "That wasn't funny."

"What, sweetie? Are you okay?"

"No, I'm not okay, and I don't appreciate your tricks."

"I didn't do anything, Rob."

"Of course not." He tossed the skis into the boat, then pulled himself up on the ladder. He yanked on the lifejacket buckles and threw the vest on the floor. He grabbed a towel, wrapping it around his white, lean body. Dan jumped in while David took over driving the boat. Teresa held the flag, ignoring the battle going on across from her.

"You don't have any *facts*, Rob," Carolyn said. "How can you make a judgment?"

"It's obvious what happened, and I'm telling you, I don't appreciate it."

"You need to *relax* when you ski. You're too stiff. Have some fun."

"I was having fun until you pulled your cute trick."

Carolyn looked at him and smiled, catty and satisfied. She reached for the cooler. "Want something to drink?"

Carolyn's day ended before she could shake her frustrations, or gather the fragments of her mind back together.

Joann surprised everyone by being true to her word that she could barbecue not only edible, but good ribs. She piled them high on the cloth-covered picnic table, surrounded by corn on the cob that came out tough and waterlogged, and sweet cantaloupe. A cooling breeze blew across the deck as they ate.

Carolyn avoided Rob, laughing over the day's events with Joann and Teresa. She smiled at him several times for the benefit of everyone else. She knew he pretended not to see her. She didn't care. She could play the game even if he couldn't. *Let everyone else think he is a foolish, unforgiving child.*

A few times she noticed David put his arm around Joann. Joann didn't melt into him as she used to. She didn't even look at him when he complimented her cooking. In the middle of dessert, Joann ran to

David, throwing her arms around him and kissing him like a new beau. *I'll never figure her out.*

Joann insisted on cleaning up alone. She returned with blue envelopes, each tied with a silver ribbon. She gave one to each person. Carolyn turned hers over once, trying to decide what made it soft and squishy inside. She lifted the flap to find a stuffed crocheted heart. A note written on blue paper said:

"To my friend of the heart. This is to remind you that I treasure our special friendship in my heart."

Carolyn's eyes filled with tears. As she hugged Joann, Teresa joined them.

The men thanked her for the crocheted cars. Joann laughed. "I didn't want to leave you guys out, so I thought I'd make a Christmas ornament for your tree."

The awkwardness dissipated. Everyone said their good-byes.

Rob and Carolyn wore painted smiles as they drove down the driveway, waving at their friends standing on the deck. At the bottom of the hill, Rob turned to Carolyn. "How dare you make a fool out of me this afternoon."

Carolyn looked out her window, thinking of a Scarlett O'Hara answer that would likely send him into a complete rage. She decided against it, saying instead, "Oh, Rob, cool off, would you? You had fun the rest of the day, didn't you?"

"Yes, as soon as I decided to pretend you weren't there."

"Grow up. Can't you take a joke?"

"I can take a joke. But you didn't mean it as a joke."

"Forget it."

"I can't forget it. You humiliated me." Rob turned the car in the driveway. He shut off the engine, grabbing her wrist as she started to get out. His voice softened. "Please don't do it again, Carolyn. I don't carry much pride. But what I do have, I'd like you to protect."

She gave him a quizzical look. He kissed her, then got out of the car. She waited until he reached the porch before she opened her door.

A stirring in her told her to tell him she loved him. She ignored it, hoping he'd stew a while longer.

·16·

oann walked through the park, feeling like a mother duck. She hoped no one watched as the ducks walked beside her, everyone waddling in rhythm. From her distance she saw Vicki involved in talking to a group of guys that hung around her. She put her head on the short one's shoulder. She did a little dance step to another and gave him a hug. Then she held both Martin's hands, stood on her tiptoes, and kissed him.

A boat pulled up, the group waved at Vicki, dashed to the water, and climbed in the boat. Martin blew her a kiss as the boat sped off.

Joann walked up behind her. "Don't you think you're too friendly with all the guys, Vicki?"

"Hey, hi!" Vicki sat on top of a table. "Don't worry about me. I've got everything under control."

"I am worried about you," Joann said, easing herself onto the bench.

"You don't realize the things you do are telling them something you don't mean."

"Like what?"

"Putting your arms around them, teasing, batting those butterfly lashes. I've even heard you say, 'Hey, let's party sometime.' To them that means something far different than you mean."

"Oh," Vicki said with a wave of her hand. "They know me. I don't party like *that*."

"I know that, and you know that. But when you tell them you want to party, drugs, booze, and sex are the norm for them."

"Don't play mother, Joann. I can take care of myself." She shaded her eyes, scanning the lake for a blue jet boat.

"I'm afraid you'll get yourself into a situation where you can't get out."

"School starts next week."

"Don't avoid the subject."

"I don't want to talk about it anymore."

"Okay. One more thing. If you ever need help, call me. Anytime."

"You'll never hear from me."

"Fine. But don't forget it."

* * *

Bible studies, baby showers, and Tupperware parties passed in quick succession. Joann loved to socialize, catching up on the needs of the people in her community. She made mental notes of who she could help, and how. She loved lining baskets with country-print fabric, stuffing them full of needed food items, then dropping them off on doorsteps.

At the baby showers for the women at church she listened to every detail of the delivery stories that sounded like a "Can you top this?" game. She planned to be fully prepared for this birth. She wanted to savor every precious minute.

After the first few parties, she began to choose a seat away from Carolyn. She tired of hearing about the horrors of abortion, and grieved over the longing that filled Carolyn's eyes during the delivery stories. She wanted to fill that void for Carolyn, with a touch, a word of hope, something to make the hurt go away. *Continued failure is a hard thing to live with,* she thought. *And I'm tired of failing.* So she sat between women she didn't know well.

Teresa attended some of the parties, looking uncomfortable, yet tolerant. Once, she had leaned over to Joann, saying, "I hate these things."

"Then why do you come?" Joann whispered back.

Teresa looked down a moment before answering. "I have enough Tupperware to last until I'm eighty, I hate the inane conversation at showers . . . I guess I come only to show the hostess or guest that I love her. If they only knew how much love it takes to get me here."

Joann put her hand on Teresa's, signaling her to be quiet. The mother-to-be placed Joann's gift on her lap, preparing to open it. Joann came ultimately for this moment. She lost her feeling of ineptness with the look of appreciation and the oohs and aahs as the gift rounded the circle. For these few moments, she could have pride in herself.

Joann's turn to be honored arrived in mid-September, with only a month to go before the baby's due date. Carolyn and Teresa hosted the shower, decorating Carolyn's house with pink and blue balloons, yellow crepe streamers, and a large bakery cake with a frosting buggy on top.

Delivery stories, as usual, were passed around along with the opened gifts. With each gift, Joann tried unsuccessfully to steer some of the conversation in another direction for her childless friends. Teresa looked grateful. Carolyn seemed numb.

Joann received many handmade gifts. She tried not to cringe at the sloppy, sometimes ugly work. She fingered each as though it were elegant, and thanked the giver.

As she opened the final card, the words written on it struck deep within her. "For your first baby . . ." The lie she lived swept over her. She looked around the room at the fresh, innocent faces surrounding her. Did any of them hurt as she did? Had any of them scraped away untimely tissue? Did they suffer for doing right?

She turned to the pastor's wife, who gave her a set of crib sheets. Her voice sounded wooden. "Thank you very much. Your kindness is overwhelming."

She hoped everyone thought her voice sounded choked up because of gratitude.

* * *

The darkness swirled. Joann moaned. The nightmare tried to begin and stopped in confusion, drowned by the pain. Joann woke, her abdomen hard as a rock, the swelling pain beginning to subside. Six minutes later, it began again. Tightening . . . squeezing . . . forcing her to breathe in careful measured breaths as she had practiced for the past eight weeks.

She spent the next hour walking round and round the living room, stopping every six minutes with her hand resting on the back of David's favorite chair.

At 4:13, she touched David, pulling the pillow from his head. "Babe," she whispered, "it's time for us to go."

"Go where?" David groaned, rolling over and grabbing the pillow.

"The hospital. I'm in labor."

"Can you wait till morning?" he asked, still groggy.

"David, come on."

The insistence in Joann's voice woke David fully. He shook his head to get his blood moving. "Do I have enough time to take a shower?"

"A quick one."

"You ready?"

"Almost."

The emergency room sent for an OB nurse and a wheelchair to help Joann to the delivery floor. Once there, David helped her out of her clothes and into a hospital gown. All dignity fled. Joann needed each available helping hand to move, to get on and off the bed.

As the pains grew stronger, Joann struggled to continue. David reminded her to keep the rhythm of her breathing in an attempt to minimize the excruciating pain. He held her hand, stroked her hair, ran errands for her. He told her again and again how much he loved her, how proud he was of her, and quoted verses of strength in her ear.

She clung to him and to his strength. She had heard of women who shouted their husbands out of the room during labor. She pleaded with him not to leave. She had been told of the bonding that takes place with the baby, but no one had told her of the wonderful bonding that took place with her husband.

In the delivery room, he held her up, encouraged her to push, to give all her strength for their child.

At 10:10 A.M. on October 24, Nicole Elizabeth was born. As the doctor laid her on Joann's stomach, their tears began to flow. David kissed Joann through his mask. He pulled it up, and kissed her again.

A nurse wrapped Nicole in a warm blanket, giving her to Joann. Joann kissed each finger, stroked the fine, wet, black hair, crying all the while. Nicole stared at her mother with big black eyes. David stroked Joann's hair, while he talked to his new daughter.

He carried Nicole back to the labor room, while the nurse pushed Joann's gurney.

David called everyone they knew while Joann nursed the baby. She couldn't get over the sense of awe, of accomplishment. God had finally blessed. He had finally forgiven.

I will never let you out of my sight, my little one.

The next morning, tears fell on the baby as Joann nursed her. She rocked on painful stitches in the hospital bed, holding the baby tight. "Nicole, Nicole, why didn't I know how precious a baby is? How alive, how real?"

The door opened, and Joann wiped her eyes with the back of her hand. "David, I'm so glad you came."

"Carolyn and Rob are here too, but the nurses won't let them in until you are done feeding the baby."

His face beamed.

"What are you so pleased about?" she asked him.

"Nicole. What a beautiful baby." He sat on the hospital bed, and stroked Nicole. "I never knew what an incredible thing it is to watch a baby nurse. My baby."

Joann touched his arm. "David. Thanks for all your help yesterday. You will never know how much you helped. I love you so much."

* * *

Nicole's perfect room welcomed her at home the next day. A Saturday. A rainy day. A mobile of clouds and angels came alive over her cradle, in the rare moment Joann placed her there. She slept through the coos of visitors and pettings of Mother. She wet, cried, burped, and ate.

And the pain in Joann's chest tormented her. She locked it all away in a closet marked "No Other Choice" and knew she had done the best she could at the time.

Carolyn's first visit to Nicole coincided with Nicole's first hour at home. She didn't seem to be ashamed at the tears that washed her face. She unwrapped and wrapped Nicole several times. The scrawny arms and legs were as delicate to her as to her mother. "Joann, you are so blessed. I hope you know that."

"She is perfect, isn't she."

"Even if she wasn't. . . ."

Little pangs of jealousy touched both women. One longed for a child of her own, the other did not want to share her own gift.

"I'll take her any time you want, Joann. I mean that."

"Thanks, Carolyn. I appreciate it. But I don't think we'll need anyone to watch her. I don't think I can leave her."

"I don't blame you."

"Carolyn. Thanks again for the beautiful nightie you brought me yesterday. You didn't need to bring me anything."

"Everyone needs to feel pretty. No one can feel pretty in a hospital gown."

"That's the truth!"

Carolyn pulled the blanket tight around Nicole, then held the baby to her shoulder, rocking slightly from side to side. "If you change your mind, Auntie Carolyn will be right over." She kissed the soft cheek, and with tears streaming down her face, handed Nicole to Joann and left.

·17·

The steady rain soaked the small airport. Surrounded by walnut orchards, the airport backed up against the hills. David and Joann sat in the protection of the restaurant, waiting for the small plane, carrying Joann's mother, to land. David's emotions split when anticipating this visit. He knew Joann needed her mother's help through at least one exhausting week. He also knew her mother was anxious to hold her first grandchild. He knew too, she wanted to be a part of the beginning of this life. But the other side of David saw an intruder in his house. Another person to take Joann's attention. He consoled himself that it would only last a week, and anyone could tolerate a week. He sipped his coffee, staring out into the rain.

Joann stared alternately into her tea, then at the sky. She longed for her mother's approval. Her mother demanded perfection, and Joann worried about her massive imperfections. She held Nicole, unaware of how tightly she clutched her.

Yet she was excited, too. Excited to hand her mother the perfect baby she had produced.

The plane touched down ten minutes late. David and Joann pushed their chairs back. Joann picked up the diaper bag and her purse, still clutching Nicole. David dropped a dollar bill and a couple of quarters on the table. Downstairs, the passengers dashed through the rain to an open pavilion, the only "terminal" at the airport.

The last woman off the plane scanned the crowd. She dashed through the rain. In a flurry of tears, kisses, and hugs, the greetings were made, Nicole revealed, and Grandma held her first grandbaby.

Nicole's first bath was accomplished with a good deal of fear from both mother and baby. Grandma looked on, laughing. "Joann, cradle your arm underneath her back, and through her arm. That's right."

"But, Mom, I'm so afraid of her slipping out."

"Like little fresh-caught fish, they are. You'll get used to it."

Dried, lotioned, powdered, and diapered, exhausted Nicole fell asleep. Grandma patted Nicole's back for a minute, before leaving the room. "Whenever you girls got fussy, I'd give you a bath," she told Joann. "It never failed to put you to sleep. You were the cleanest babies around."

"Aren't babies precious, Mom?"

"Sure. And sometimes a precious pain."

A look of shock passed over Joann's face. "What do you mean, a pain? Nicole is special. A gift. She will never leave my arms."

"Joann, you will want to have time to yourself."

"Not me, Mom. She'll go with me wherever I go. I want her to know how much she is loved."

"Don't you think love is giving and doing the best for someone else?"

"Of course. That's why I want to be with Nicole. No one else will give her the best, because they couldn't possibly love her as much as I do."

"You will have to let her go sometime. To friends' houses."

"Her friends will come here to play."

"To school."

"I am thinking I will school her at home."

"When she gets married, or goes to college, or gets a job."

"Then it will be okay."

"Do you really think so, Joann? After eighteen years of being only in Mother's company, with you protecting and shielding her, do you really think it will be okay for her to do anything on her own? I don't think you could let her go. Besides, there is another danger in holding her so tight."

"What kind of danger can there be in loving and protecting your child?"

"The danger of her not knowing now to cope in the world. Not knowing how to deal with disappointments, temptations, and fears."

"Home will always be here as a refuge."

Grandma shook her head, throwing her hands in the air. "I wish I knew where you got these crazy ideas, Joann. They aren't healthy."

"Did you ever think, Mother, that your relationship with us wasn't healthy? You were so tied up with being perfect for others, you forgot to be nice to us at home."

"Joann, I know I wasn't a very good mother, but for you to swing to the other extreme scares me."

"Well, don't be scared, Mom. She'll be the best kid you ever met."

The rest of the week passed in mounds of diapers, sloshes of baths, burpings and urpings, and conversation about babies and doings, without ever again talking about rearing Nicole. Grandma cleaned the house, washed the dishes, and made the meals. Joann cried the day she left, wondering how she'd do it all alone.

Gusts of wind blew fat raindrops at the window, sounding like someone throwing handfuls of pebbles. Joann woke from her nap, stretching and feeling a moment of delicious confusion. It didn't matter what day it was, or where or who she might be. The smell of fresh-baked chocolate-chip cookies caught her attention. *I didn't make any cookies*, she thought.

She found Vicki and David in the living room, a plate of cookies perched on a TV tray. "Hi, sleepyhead," David said.

"I thought you only took naps when you were pregnant," Vicki stated.

"I did, too. The doctor says delivery takes a lot out of you."

"Not to mention the two A.M. and five A.M. feedings," David added.

"You love excuses, don't you, Joann?" Vicki said.

Vicki put two cookies on a napkin and handed them to Joann, one obviously overdone, the other, underdone. "They still don't look like yours, do they, Joann?"

"Not quite, but you're getting there."

"I figured you wouldn't be making any for a while, so I thought I'd better make some before David went into withdrawal."

"I'm glad somebody's worrying about me," David said.

Joann flashed a "better be quiet" look.

"So what terribly exciting conversation did I interrupt?" Joann asked.

"You're right," Vicki said, "nothing terribly exciting."

"I was asking Vicki about her future. But she won't answer."

"What's to answer?"

"What do you want to do when you grow up?" David persisted.

"I'll never grow up, so there's nothing to worry about."

"Come on, Vick, you must have thought of something."

"Maybe a lawyer," Vicki said.

"No, Vicki, no," David protested. "You'd never win a case."

"No kidding," Joann said. "You'd always feel sorry for the defendant and give in to him."

"Yeah, but they make lots of money."

David rolled his eyes while Joann moaned.

"Maybe I'll just be a zoo keeper instead. Or go to that clown school in Florida. I've got lots of years left before I decide. Besides, did you know you wanted to be a housewife with kids when you were in high school?" Vicki asked Joann.

"Well, no."

"See. I don't need to make any decisions."

David laughed. "You're hopeless."

"That's what my mother always says. Oh, Joann, let *me* get Nicole."

Joann reluctantly agreed. With the first whimper, she had been half out of the chair. Vicki must have been waiting for the moment. Joann did follow Vicki into the nursery, clucking instructions. "Remember to hold her head. We've got to change the diaper. Why don't you let me."

"Will you just get out?"

"I'll just watch."

Vicki nodded at each instruction, continuing to do things in her own way. "Hi there, little Nikki," she cooed.

"Don't call her Nikki. I don't like that."

"Then why'd you name her Nicole? Oh, the sweet little baby."

"Joann," David called. "Come here for a minute."

The anxious mother backed out of the nursery, then trotted into the living room. "What?"

"Come over here and sit on my lap."

"But I have to stay. . . ."

"Nicole is in capable hands."

"But what if she drops her."

"Nicole is okay, now come here. I've forgotten what it's like to have a wife."

"I'm sorry, David. I've been so tied up. . . ."

"I wish you'd get a little less tied up."

She snuggled into the comfort of David's lap. She had forgotten, in her preoccupation with Nicole, how strengthened she felt there. A tiny whimper came from the bedroom, and she stiffened. "Relax, Joann," David said. "Everything's okay."

Vicki appeared, and sat in the rocking chair. She sang a soft lullaby in Nicole's ear. Nicole rooted around Vicki's neck, searching for the source of her deepest pleasure.

"I know," David whispered. "She ought to be a nanny."

Joann hated to admit it, but clumsy, sloppy Vicki seemed right at home with a newborn on her shoulder.

For a moment, full and happy, Joann's life was as it should be.

Soon the rooting became furious, interspersed with fitful wails. Joann took Vicki's place, and the wails changed to tiny gulps and little sighs.

Joann wondered at this new little person formed from the love of two people. It seemed too awesome to understand. A comfortable silence listened to the baby.

·18·

..The November moon rose over the mountains, casting its silver path along the lake. Little Harbor Inn sat on the edge of the lake. A small marina gathered around it, the boats rocking softly in the water. Music seeped into the dining room from the lounge where people danced, drank, and picked out partners for the night. Inside the dining room, candlelight lit up faces, intensifying each emotion. The Inn's formal atmosphere made it a favorite place for the local teenagers to bring a date they wanted to impress. Several of them were scattered about the room now, obvious in their awkward silences and casual, stilted conversations.

A smattering of retirees and young couples occupied the other tables. Dan smiled at Teresa, reaching across the table to hold her hand. "When are you going to go and see the new baby?" he asked.

Teresa looked down at her plate, picking at the swordfish with her fork. "You know how I feel about babies, Dan."

"This one is special to you, isn't it?" he said gently, his hand stroking hers.

"Joann is special. But I don't know how I'll feel when I see the baby."

"Sad? Angry? Those are okay feelings. But maybe you won't feel that way at all."

"I'm only scared now."

"What reason have you given Joann for not going over yet?"

"I told her I didn't want to wear her out since everyone else in this town seems to have tromped through there. She laughed and said I was different, so I said the real reason was, I refused to come until I finished Nicole's gift."

"Have you finished it?"

"Last week."

Dan chewed on his steak, thinking. "You know, I always remember her kindness to us when we moved in. And all her kindnesses since then. The wall hanging she made is perfect for over the couch. She sees needs and fills them, like the fancy hotpads she made after she saw how you scorched ours. Or making meals for new mothers. I even saw her giving an old lady—you know Mrs. Randolph?—a quilt! That lady dresses so shabbily, Joann must have figured she needed warmth and beauty in her life." He paused to stuff a chunk of french bread into his mouth. "Hers is the most sincere friendship I've seen. You haven't had a friend in so long, Teresa. Don't lose this one now."

Teresa sipped her Perrier. "Do you think I push friends away?"

"Sometimes. I think you do everything you can to have them not be your friends, to give them reasons to spend less time with you. Why are you so afraid of their finding out?"

"I don't want to get into this again, Dan."

"You can't hide forever, Teresa."

"I know, Dan. Let's just drop it, okay?"

Her dinner had been ruined. The glistening fish now made her queasy, instead of hungry. Then Dan started telling her some new funny mail-delivery stories which soon had her laughing. She watched his face scrunch up to be an old codger or turn delicate to match that of a small child, as he related each part of the story.

She loved him. She no longer saw his constant pushing back of the greasy hair determined to drop into his face. Nor did she try to get him to buy a pair of stylish glasses. "I would rather spend the money to take you out to dinner," he would say. And he did.

She loved who he was. His challenges to her, his understanding when she failed. She thought of him as a buried treasure, which is never pretty, but stuck all over with barnacles. "You just have to know what you are looking for," her mother had told her. Teresa had known what she looked for, and Dan didn't fit the description. If she hadn't been stuck with him on that blind date, she never would have agreed to go out with him.

She looked into his candlelit face and smiled. "Thank God for blind dates," she whispered.

"What?" asked Dan.

"I'm thanking God for blind dates."

"I do every day."

* * *

The next day, Teresa decided to see Nicole after church. Each week she had asked Joann if she planned to take the baby to church. Teresa wouldn't go if the baby would be there. Today she didn't need to call. She would spend the morning making some casseroles to put in Joann's freezer. Joann hated to cook for herself, and Teresa hated to think that Nicole would be nourished off TV dinners.

As she cooked, she prayed for herself—for kindness, love for the baby, and that she wouldn't panic.

She made several trips to Joann's front door, piling up her gifts. With the last casserole in her hand, she rang the doorbell. David answered, his friendly smile getting bigger when he saw the food. "Well, now. A woman after my own heart."

Joann came up behind him. "Teresa!" When she saw the three casseroles and the gift, her eyes grew big, her mouth fell open. "What is all this?"

David scooped up two casseroles after balancing the gift on top of Teresa's covered dish. "What do you think it is, silly. It's food for the hungry."

"We're not hungry."

"Speak for yourself." He put the casserole dishes on the kitchen table, then lifted the lids to see inside. Teresa set hers down too, then turned to hand Joann the present.

Joann took it, gesturing to Teresa to follow her. "Come sit down. I can't believe you did all this. You didn't have to, you know."

"I hated thinking of the baby getting TV dinners for nutrition."

David laughed, Joann looked embarrassed. "I'm trying to cook more when David is gone. It's hard to cook for one."

116

"That's why I decided to cook a few dinners for you."

Joann's voice grew soft. "Thanks so much, Teresa."

"Where's Nicole?"

"She's in bed. She'll be up in a few minutes, I bet. It's almost time for her to eat."

As Joann pulled the paper off the gift, Teresa felt butterflies swooping around her stomach. Her feet rubbed against each other, and she clenched her teeth, concentrating on Joann and the gift.

"Teresa, I love it!" Joann said as she lifted a framed counted cross-stitch from the box. Nicole's name and birth date, length and weight, were stitched in the center. Around the border floated a ribbon, held by a little bear sitting in the bottom corner. Flowers intertwined with the ribbon.

"I'll never be as good as you," Teresa said.

"But I can't do counted cross-stitch. This is beautiful."

"Do you have anything like that?"

"No. I hadn't gotten around to making anything yet. But this is better than what I had in mind. So much better." Joann got up from the chair and went over to give Teresa a hug. "Thanks for the casseroles too."

Joann started. "Oh, there's Nicole, I'll be back in a second."

Teresa looked at David. "I didn't hear anything, did you?"

"No. Joann has ultrasensitive ears when it comes to Nicole."

Joann called from the bedroom. "Teresa, why don't you come in here while I change Nicole."

"I think I'll just wait here," she called back, hoping Joann wouldn't detect the fear in her voice.

Joann appeared a few moments later carrying a bundle of blanket. She proudly walked over to Teresa, laying the bundle in her lap. Teresa stiffened, her arms refusing to hold the baby.

"Isn't she precious?" Joann crooned, unaware of Teresa's awkwardness.

Teresa forced herself to look at the baby. Her body softened, and she lifted the baby up to her shoulder. Nicole's soft sweet baby smell and tiny sucking noises touched the mother inside Teresa. She put her hand behind Nicole's head, and rocked her back and forth, her cheek resting against the downy soft head.

Suddenly feeling self-concious, she pulled Nicole down to cradle her in her arms, and to get a better look at her. Tears welled up in her eyes, a few spilling over. *It's so different,* she thought. Then the old feelings came back. "Here," she said to Joann. "I don't feel real comfortable with babies. Actually I'm kind of scared of them."

Joann laughed. "You didn't look very scared to me. You're a natural."

"I'm not, really I'm not," she protested. "I think I'd better go now."

"It's okay, you can stay while I feed her."

"I'd better get home. Dan and I always do something together on Sunday afternoons."

David looked up from the massive Sunday paper. "I like to do things with Joann on Sunday afternoons too."

Joann give him a dirty look. Then she turned to Teresa. "Thanks again, Teresa. I really appreciate it."

"So do I," David said.

Teresa went out on the deck, rather than inside her apartment. She pulled a chair up to the rail, sitting back, and putting her feet up on the railing. She felt drained and guilty. As if expecting a storm, the lake had turned a deep gray, swollen and choppy. Clouds collected against the mountains on the north side of the lake. A cold wind blew across the deck, but Teresa didn't feel it. She sat, not feeling anything, except heavy. No thoughts came into her blank mind. She stared at the lake, and then at her own soul.

She knew she had done wrong. She knew it now, but she didn't know it then. It was only a job then. A compassionate job, helping other women. They hurt so bad when they came in, they were so relieved when they left.

Her jaws began to chew on an invisible piece of gum. *Sweet, soft, clean-smelling Nicole.* Happiness flooded that house. Why did life have to be this way? Why did mistakes have to be made? Why can't we always do what is right?

You were ignorant, her mind defended.

I was stupid.

You didn't know.

It took me so long to figure it out.

But when you did, you left.

After two more weeks. I stayed two more weeks thinking it must be right somewhere. TWO MORE WEEKS. Why didn't I walk out that very moment? Why didn't I tell anyone why I left? A weakling, that's all I am.

Yes, you are.

Thanks a lot. I needed your support.

The sliding glass door opened. Dan stuck his head out. "Are you okay?"

Teresa shook her head.

"Anything I can do to help?"

She shrugged her shoulders.

"Shall we go somewhere?"

"Yes. Let's go for a hike somewhere. I need to see the best of God's creation. I can only remember what I did to destroy it."

Dan came over, kneeling down beside her. "You didn't destroy it. The doctors did."

"I was the assistant. I helped."

"You helped the women."

"That doesn't excuse it."

"No, it doesn't. But someday God will use what you know to help others."

"I'm so ashamed. I scream at myself for my ignorance. How can anyone be so ignorant in an abortion hospital? How come I didn't *see* until they moved me to second trimesters? Not until I saw those babies. I only saw blood before. Nothing else. I only saw hurting faces, leaving relieved. I thought I did a service. Oh, God, help me. I destroyed lives. I was part of it."

Dan cuddled his sobbing wife, stroking her hair. "I love you, Teresa. God loves you. He understands, He forgives. He can use it. He really can."

Teresa's sobs melted away. "Let's go on that hike. I don't want to think about this anymore."

·19·

.·David's hands flew as the ends of the lettuce dropped into a box. He whisked off the wilted leaves, then wrapped the lettuce in the accordion plastic wrap. His mind raced as fast as his hands.

He hated the feelings that controlled him these days. Like a child, jealousy and anger burned through him at being shut out. Joann had time for everyone but him. The hurting and needy of the town sang her praises at how she gave of herself so willingly to them. She tied up every waking moment in someone else, usually Nicole.

Old, ugly feelings came back, remnants of his ninth summer. His best friend, John, laughed at him when he struck out with the bases loaded during a crucial Little League game. John then took off with the team's star hitter, leaving David without a friend. The rejection hurt. And it hurt now.

He could go home to tell Joann how he had been promoted again, but she would be too interested in how much Nicole had spit up, and how long she slept, or, oh, my goodness, look at that smile. In the store's history, no one had ever been promoted twice in one year. David shared it with Dan, who slapped him on the back and pumped his hand. Rob smiled at him. "It's no surprise to me, David. You're the best. You'll have charge of that department in no time."

Dan's exuberance and Rob's praise reassured the confidence David had in his work. But he could not help but hurt. Joann's hands could create a work of art, but her ears could not hear anything but Nicole's cry.

Every waking moment, David and Nicole heard never-ending coos and love talk. When Nicole slept, the phone seemed glued to Joann's ear as she chattered to everyone, filling them in on the details of the little angel's life.

David hated himself for resenting Nicole. Many a night he wished she had never been born. When morning came, the resentment had disappeared. Her life, to him too, was a joy.

He loved to hold her, and play with her. He could watch TV, and let her fall asleep on his chest. In public, he carried her like a trophy. He loved her dearly, but he wanted a wife, too. A partner to share his joy.

David didn't know whether to stay away, or spend time at home whenever he could. While away, he missed Joann. While home, he missed Joann, but her physical presence and mental absence frustrated and infuriated him. So he gave himself to work, and they promoted him ahead of the others to be right-hand man to Mr. Saito.

The librarians began to recognize him, as he came in to read the reference books about produce, and order others from the library's lending network program. He had never been a reader, but marketing and handling of produce interested him. It hurt to see Joann didn't notice his absence. She didn't question where he went or what he did.

He withdrew from her, and they didn't laugh much anymore, unless they were with their friends.

He wheeled his boxes of lettuce out to the rack, and began stacking them.

"David!"

"Vicki! Isn't this Tuesday? Aren't you supposed to be with Joann?"

"Ehh. She isn't all that good to be with anymore. She spends too much time hugging Nicole. She wasn't paying attention to what I was doing. So I told her I had homework to do."

David nodded, trying not to seem as if he agreed with her.

"How's Martin?"

"Martin's terrific, as usual. We went to Mendocino last Saturday."

"Beautiful place, isn't it?"

"Yeah. I really like it. It was pretty cold, but I like it that way too."

"Had Martin ever been there?"

"Nope. He's a Southern California beach bum, so the whole thing shocked him pretty much. He thought of the whole coast as one solid beach from Canada through Mexico."

David smiled; he didn't want to admit he and Joann had the same misconception.

"He didn't like the town all that much. I don't think he's into artists and quaint stuff. He's got expensive tastes. But I don't care. We went to a very expensive restaurant. The food was the best I've ever had."

"What's the name of the place?"

"Who pays attention? Martin chooses, Martin pays, I just watch Martin."

David laughed. "True love at its worst. The world passes by, and nothing matters but his face." David put up the last head of lettuce. "I'd better get the apples. Back in a sec. Will you wait?"

"Okay."

David stacked apple boxes on the cart in the back room, including one empty to put the old apples in.

He liked Vicki. A little sister to watch out for, tease, and talk to.

"Will your folks let you go to church yet?" he asked her when he returned.

"No. I don't dare ask anymore. Dad blew up and threw a beer bottle across the room the last time I asked. Joann gives me a Bible-study lesson like she gets, so I do that sometimes. It's a little over my head though," she whispered.

David smiled. "That's okay. Just so long as you and God keep in touch."

"Hey, we're buddies!"

David laughed. Vicki gave him fresh insight into God and having a relationship with Him. It made him thankful for the program at her high school that was showing her that she could have a relationship with God.

"What time is it, David?"

"Four-thirty."

"Oh, hey, hate to leave you, but Prince Charming is waiting to buy me something to spoil my dinner."

"Thanks for stopping by, Vick."

Her braid flew in the air as she whirled around. She stuck her arm in the air, waving her hand around. "Byeee!"

He shook his head as Philip, another produce clerk said, "That girl is crazy."

"She's a special crazy."

"Plain crazy."

With Christmas only two weeks away, David felt he should be happier. He and Joann planned to visit their families in Southern California. He hoped he could recapture some threads of contentment and happiness while there. And maybe the drive down would bring Joann closer to him. They always talked better when they took long trips together.

* * *

David rubbed the gearshift knob, then tapped his fingers on it. Only two more hours to go. His mom would be waiting, anxious to see her grandchild. The house would smell of hot wassail and fresh Christmas tree. His dad, the couch potato, would change channels on the television at every commercial, while still being involved in the commotion.

He tried to focus on the warmth of home while Nicole screamed in his ear. He thought about screaming with her or at her. He didn't blame her for hating the car seat after eight hours, but forty-five minutes of straight screaming was too much. Joann's attitude didn't help him either. His attempts to get close failed. He tried touching her hand. It felt like a mannequin's. When Nicole quieted down, he again tried several different approaches to conversation.

"Have you thought any more about teaching women how to quilt?"

"No. I'm so busy with Nicole, I can't see where I'd find the time."

"A few months ago you looked forward to it."

"I know. But I've found Nicole more fulfilling than I ever dreamed. I don't need that now to feel good about myself."

"Will you still teach Vicki?"

"Hmm? Oh, I suppose. I'm so busy, I think I'll have to cut back on the time."

"When was the last time you saw her?"

"A couple of weeks ago."

"I think you need to talk to her."

"About what?"

David rubbed the steering wheel. "I can't put my finger on it, but she seems to be getting a little depressed. She usually talks to me in her crazy way. Now she talks with her head down, in a soft voice."

"Did she break up with Martin?"

"No. She said he's fine. But I think something isn't fine with their relationship."

The baby needed to be nursed then. And when Joann nursed, conversation died.

Later he tried to get her to listen to him tell her about work. She paid attention to a last-minute Christmas gift instead. He tried to talk to her about their relationship. She laughed at his concern, patting him on his knee. "David, there is no one in this world I'd rather be married to. Don't be such a worrier. What time did you tell your mom we'd be there?"

With only half an hour's driving time left, David noticed Joann seemed nervous. She kept running her fingers through her hair and staring out the window into the darkness. Her head turned to look at each exit sign. At one point, she burst into tears.

David reached his arm around her shoulder, trying to pull her close. She pulled away, her face in both hands. The sobs ended as abruptly as they started. Joann pulled a tissue from her purse and blew her nose. She sat up, and snuggled next to David.

"What was that all about?" he asked her.

Her voice, barely audible, said, "I don't know. It felt so strange. All of a sudden I remembered . . . that was the exit I took . . ." her voice died away.

"Why'd you pull away from me?"

She looked out the window. "I guess I felt for a moment that I didn't deserve you, or that you hate me, or some such dumb thing."

"You're right. It's dumb." He squeezed her shoulder as she lay her head against him.

* * *

Christmas and all the days surrounding it were nothing short of a disappointment. David thought he was as welcome as elevator music in the background. Joann and Nicole were the center of attention. *It's as if fathers aren't important for anything but making the baby. Then cast aside, used merchandise.* Joann made fun of him when he told her his feelings one night in bed. At that moment, he decided he would no longer communicate his feelings to her. She would have to change, to break down somehow before he'd ever open himself up to her again.

Their ride home was silent except for the radio and the demands of the baby.

124

·20·

  ··Joann pulled the drapes against the icy cold January night. The storm had passed, leaving crisp stars in the blackened sky, as black as Joann's spirit. She shivered, bouncing Nicole and patting her back. "It's bedtime, sugar bear. Time for your good-night song."

As she sang the song, she began to cry. Singing the good-night song, meant just for Nicole, started the tears. Tender sweetness opened the door to all the pain, all the frustration locked inside.

Joann wiped away the tears, scolding herself for being silly and sentimental. She put Nicole in her bed, pulling a quilt over her. She put her hand on Nicole's back, letting it lay there awhile. She wanted another baby. Another two, another three, lots of babies to fill her life with love. To hold, nurture, care for. There would never be enough children, she thought.

She hated to leave Nicole alone in the room. Ever since she had moved the cradle out of their bedroom when Nicole was two months old, she missed her and wondered if Nicole missed her too.

She hadn't wanted to move Nicole out, but David insisted. "I can't feel comfortable being intimate with you while Nicole is in here," he said.

"She's so little," Joann replied. "She doesn't know."

"I don't care if she knows. I know, and I don't like a third party around. It inhibits my style, you know?"

Joann laughed, and she moved the baby to her own room the next day. But she did it with a few tears.

She took her hand off Nicole's back. She hated being so weepy and hoped the postpartum blues would be over soon. Her friends told her she should have been over the blues weeks ago. A vague depression began the first time she felt Nicole kick inside of her, and hadn't let go yet. What a nuisance!

She hated, too, her jealousy whenever anyone else held Nicole. Worse, sometimes Nicole would stop crying when Carolyn held her. Carolyn talked such silly baby talk to her. Her voice changed pitch and suddenly she had no decent vocabulary or grammar.

Sometimes Nicole seemed to prefer David. Joann didn't like that either. She wanted Nicole to love her first. After all, she did give Nicole more time, love, attention, and care than anyone else.

Joann arranged the new stuffed animals around Nicole's bed so she could see them when she awoke in the night. Christmas had been fun, opening all the presents for Nicole—tiny dresses, shoes, a woolly lamb and a blue and green elephant. Nicole had slept through the whole thing, and woke at the end, when dinner was served, wanting her own dinner.

David acted worse than the baby, pouting because no one gave him any attention. She told him so too.

Carolyn had come by the day after they got home, carrying a gift box that didn't look like it came from any department store Joann shopped at. She scolded Carolyn for breaching their agreement about Christmas gifts.

"I didn't breach anything," Carolyn said. "This is for Nicole. I made no promises about Nicole."

For a moment the world stood still. Inside the box, encased in tissue paper, lay the yellow tiered dress she had picked out at Macy's. "Carolyn, I told you not to," Joann said as she admired the dress.

"And I told you I would." Carolyn wore her smug smile, so much a part of her face when she did something she knew was terrific.

Joann jumped up and threw her arms around Carolyn. "You're such a special friend."

"Don't I know it," she said.

"I want to put it on Nicole right now."

"Good luck. I bought it large so she could wear it when she's walking. I couldn't bear to see her crawling on those ruffles and ruining them, if she *could* crawl in a dress anyway."

"Sometimes I think *you* ought to be the mother, not me. I never thought of that."

"I wish I was too," Carolyn murmured.

Joann offered her a cup of tea. They laughed over a silly old movie, filmed in San Francisco. They both loved *What's Up Doc?* Carolyn pointed out one scene shot near an area where she passed out pamphlets.

"Oh, Carolyn, can't you drop it?"

"Why?"

"I'm so sick of spending time with you when the conversation somehow turns toward your work."

"What's wrong with that?"

"Maybe I feel you are getting very single-minded."

"We've got to make our stand known and fight for the lives of all the little babies."

"What about the fear and desperation of all those women who don't want to be mothers?"

"C'mon, Joann. They're not desperate, just selfish. Cold. Some even call them murderers." Carolyn lifted her mug of tea to her lips.

Joann forced her teeth to stay together as she mentally counted to ten. "How many women have you talked to who have had an abortion?"

"None, but I've seen some on TV."

"Oh, and that will give you the whole picture?"

"It's probably an accurate picture."

Joann shook her head. "How can you be so blind, Carolyn?"

"Me, blind? You are the one with your head in the sand. You won't even talk about it!"

"Forget it, Carolyn. You have no concept of what it is like to be caught, so scared, and with no way out."

"And you do?"

Joann turned away, slamming dishes around. After a few moments, she felt more calm. "I feel our friendship is strained because of a stupid disagreement."

Carolyn's mug of herbal tea stopped its ascent. It slowly came down, invisible strings from the mug pulled on her face. Only her eyebrows raised, her voice squashed by the weight of her amazement. "Are you telling me you are *for* abortion? For *murder* of those precious little babies?"

Joann fought to keep her composure. "I never said that. You weren't listening. I don't think anyone is paying attention to the pain those women must feel. Everyone points an accusing finger at them."

Carolyn tapped her long, painted nails, color coordinated with the rest of her, on the side of her mug. She scooped up a stack of pamphlets and stuffed them in her purse as she spoke. "Well, I can see I'm getting nowhere with you."

"Carolyn. . . ."

Carolyn held up her hand. "Look. Don't say any more. I'll call you when I cool off."

The door slammed behind her.

Joann went to the corner of Nicole's room and grabbed Teddy. She hated the feelings Carolyn stirred up within her. The pain, the guilt, the ugliness. "I did what I had to do," she sobbed in Teddy's ear, feeling stupid for being such a child. "Why does she make me feel like a murderer? She has no right."

She rocked back and forth. "Oh God, You knew. You knew I had no other choice. You knew I prayed. I asked for Your help.

"It was the best way, the easiest way, the way with the least pain. No one would ever know, and my life could continue as if nothing happened. So why hasn't it? Why does it still hurt so bad? It's been six years, and it hurts worse now than ever before. God, won't You please take away the pain? The hiding? The tears? Oh God, please take it away."

* * *

Two days later, Joann bundled Nicole in a pink bunting over a pink sleeper with a T-shirt next to her skin. A blanket covered all that, making it look like a bundle of laundry had been stuffed in the stroller. Joann pushed the stroller to the post office to pick up her mail. Then she walked up the sidewalk, pushing with one hand, while checking the mail with the other. As she rounded the corner, she almost ran into Teresa and Carolyn coming out of the Main Street Cafe.

"Joann," Carolyn said immediately. "I am so sorry about the other day. I get crazy when I miss Billy so much."

Joann cocked her head, confused. "So why would that explain the other day?"

"Whenever I think of Billy, I get thinking about my work and how important it is to me. I should never have brought it up. Will you accept my apology?"

"Of course, silly. I wanted to apologize too."

"Can I say something?" Teresa asked.

Both women turned to look at her, smiling. "I'm glad to see what a true friendship you have. Are there ever times you have hard feelings and hold a grudge?"

They looked at each other a moment, then Carolyn spoke. "If there are, we certainly wouldn't tell now, would we, Joann?"

"Of course not."

*   *   *

Now, as Joann rearranged the stuffed animals, kissing Nicole good night for the sixth time, she wondered if Carolyn ever held a grudge against her. She certainly felt guilty for carrying her anger around against Carolyn. But it made her so mad sometimes, that Carolyn could be so single-minded.

She gathered up her work for the night and plopped down in front of the TV.

·21·

T··he phone rang and rang. Carolyn timed her sit-ups to coincide with each ring. When the count reached twenty-five, the ringing stopped. A moment later, it started again. When the count reached nineteen, Carolyn decided she'd answer just to get the jerk to leave her alone. She grabbed her towel, wiping the sweat from her face, angry at the interruption. She took her time getting to the phone, hoping they would hang up before she got there. She let out a gigantic sigh for the benefit of the rude caller as she lifted the receiver. "Hello. Mom? I've told you not to call between—

"Mom? Are you there? Don't cry, it's okay."

"Carolyn, it's not okay. I'm at the hospital. . . ."

"Who's sick? Dad? Is it his heart?"

"It's Billy. They. . . ."

"What, Mom, appendix? Appendix isn't much to worry about. Remember when he had his tonsils out? You were so worried then."

130

"*Carolyn!* Shut up and listen to me."

"Mom, calm down."

"They don't know if Billy's going to make it."

"What do you mean 'going to make it'?"

"They pulled him up from the bottom of the community pool." Her mom's voice struggled, turning into a squeal. "They say he ran off the high dive, flapping his arms. I think the kids encouraged him."

"The high dive?"

"Yes. Martha took him with her family so I could get his birthday present. She had to take Shelly to the bathroom. When she came out . . ." her voice quivered and broke, the words coming out like shots. "They were trying to revive him. The kids who dared him to do it were so scared they didn't tell the lifeguards when Billy didn't come up." Her words broke into sobs.

"Mom, so what are the doctors saying?"

"They don't know yet. He's in a coma. They don't know what will happen. Or when."

Neither spoke. The music played on in the background, the beat pulsing, demanding Carolyn's routine to continue.

Through a sob, Carolyn's mother spoke. "I can't talk anymore, Carolyn, I just can't."

Carolyn hung up the phone, her mind numb. "If I were a bird," she heard a little voice say.

She turned off the music.

Stepping into the shower, her thoughts and prayers began to race through the ifs, and the pleas.

If they didn't live in Los Angeles, it would never have been warm enough to swim in January. If Mom had waited to let Dad watch Billy, instead of letting him go off with someone incompetent. . . .

The water poured over her face as she ran the bar of soap over one arm again and again.

God, don't let my Billy die. Don't take away my joy, my inspiration for doing my work. Don't stop his precious smile, his bear hugs, and slobbery kisses.

Oh, God. Oh God. Oh God. Please.

She stared at the mildew starting to form in the corner of the tile wall. The water grew cold, and she stayed until she started shivering. She pulled her towel from the rack, wrapping it around her. She stood for a long time, trying to keep the panic from swelling up and choking her. "Oh God. Oh God. Oh God," she whispered again and again. *Let Billy live.*

She called Rob at work, relayed the news, and hung up before he had a chance to respond. She dressed, and sat on the couch to wait. Her thoughts flew away from her, doves released from a cage, scattering in the air, unable to be caught.

The front door opening startled her. "Oh, Rob. I'm so glad you came."

Rob sat beside her and held her, praying. He went to the phone and called the church prayer chain, Teresa, and Joann. To each he explained in short, terse words the situation. He went into the kitchen and made Carolyn a cup of tea. When he returned to her, she looked at him and smiled. "Thanks, Rob. I don't know what I'd do without you."

He kissed the top of her head, and put his arm around her. "You know, Rob, I suddenly have such peace. I know Billy's going to make it."

"Why do you think that?"

"It's the peace. It's an intuition. A knowing. You can go back to work now. I'll be fine."

"Are you sure?"

"Of course I'm sure. Now go."

"I don't know if I can work."

"Try. I don't suppose sitting around staring at each other all day is going to accomplish much. I'm going to put on my makeup and take a walk. Thank God for His answered prayer."

Rob raised his eyebrows, paused for a moment, then gathered up his overcoat and left.

Carolyn fixed herself up, then went for a walk. Part of her felt heavy, sick, and sad. Another part flew with the peace and confidence that swelled in her soul.

She walked out on an old pier, driving the sea gulls away. She stood there, watching the cold lake water churn. The sky, dark and foreboding, lowered clouds over Mount Sakar. Tiny drops of rain started to fall. Carolyn stayed until the drops came so fast she could not see twenty feet across the lake. She wandered home, looking as torn and disheveled as a bag lady.

She shed her wet clothes in the tiled entry, then turned the thermostat up to 78 degrees. She snuggled into a warm robe and slippers, curled up on the bed, and fell asleep.

The persistent phone woke her from a strange dream about Billy flying over the lake. "Hello? Joann!"

"How are you doing? Is there anything I can do?" Joann asked.

"No, I'm fine. Really. Everything's going to be okay."

She hung up the phone and glanced at the clock. "Oh, dear, I'd better get dinner. I didn't realize it was so late."

She padded into the kitchen, pulling a few things from the refrigerator. She put some leftover homemade onion soup on the stove to warm. Then she made some alfalfa sprout and chicken sandwiches on seven-grain bread.

An ugly feeling, like Jonah's worm, slithered around inside her. She prayed again, thanking God for taking care of Billy. The worm moved on, ignorant of the attempts to squelch it.

When she heard the key turn in the door, she ran to Rob, throwing her arms around him. He held her tight. "Any news?"

"Nope. No news is good news. Come on, dinner's ready."

"I'm not very hungry," Rob told her. "I'm so worried about Billy."

"I told you everything's going to be fine."

In the middle of dinner, the phone rang. Carolyn leaned back to reach the receiver. "Hi, Mom. Listen, I've got something to tell you; Billy's—"

"Honey, Billy didn't make it. The doctor said it's really better this way, there would have been so much brain damage."

"*No!* God told me Billy would be okay."

Her mother's weary voice answered. "Billy is okay. He's with God now."

Carolyn's anger lashed out at her mother. "You sound awfully happy about the whole thing."

"I'm not happy. I'm exhausted, numb. Only the truth is keeping me going."

Carolyn stood up, shouting into the phone. "God lied to me, Mom. He lied to me! I want Billy back!"

Rob wrestled the phone from her, talking quickly, then hanging up. Carolyn picked up the unfinished plates, dumped the food down the sink, rinsed them, and stuffed the dishwasher. She kicked the cupboard door shut when it wouldn't close. She backhanded Rob when he tried to get too close. With each breath she tried to stuff the tears down, smash the worm who now ate ravenously at her soul.

She picked up her car keys and purse, and slammed out of the house.

Ignoring Rob's shouts, she jumped in the car, slammed the door, and raced off. She drove to the lovers' lookout point on the south end of town. She sat above it all, the lights, the black expanse of the lake, the dark shadows of mountains surrounding the lake.

She pounded the steering wheel and cried, her heart broken at the betrayal.

God doesn't love. He gives Down's children, He takes away what is loved most, gives children to those who would throw them away, and withholds them from those who would love them the most.

"God, You are a liar. You gave me peace. You promised to make Billy better. It's not worth it, God. It's not worth it to trust You. You only cause pain."

As she yelled, the peace came again. She argued with the thoughts that came with it. Thoughts that maybe God hadn't promised her anything. That she had jumped to conclusions with the peace He gave her. She wouldn't listen to the thoughts. She'd rather be mad at God.

She drove home, limp, empty.

Rob looked nervous, his hair rumpled, the newspaper unread. He looked at her, afraid to speak. She followed his gaze to the hem of her robe, muddy and wet from her trek to the car and back again. She sat on the edge of the couch.

Rob looked at her a moment more, then spoke. "Are you okay?"

"No, I'm not okay," she snapped.

"I called everyone for you. They all want to know what they can do to help."

"Tell 'em to lay their hands on Billy and bring him back to life."

Rob looked at the floor. "They all love you, Carolyn."

Carolyn didn't answer. She stood up and walked to the bedroom, took off the robe and slippers, and crawled into bed.

Ugly and empty days followed. Billy's void left a sharp silence, slicing all the goodness out of Carolyn's life.

In the mornings, she got up, putting on her muddy-hemmed robe. She walked into the kitchen, dishes piling up in the sink, and ate jelly toast for breakfast.

The rest of the day she spent in front of the TV, watching soap operas and game shows. At night, Rob tried to catch up with the stack of dishes, and picking up the house. She ignored his stares of helplessness.

On the third day, Rob told her, "The funeral is tomorrow. I got us tickets for a nine o'clock flight tonight from Sacramento."

"You don't have to come. I don't want you to come."

"I'm going," he said firmly.

At the funeral, Carolyn sat rigid and dry-eyed. She did not speak to anyone except for the absolute necessities.

At home the next day, the doorbell rang. She ignored the first two rings, then got up, answering the third. As she looked at Joann's sad face, she slammed the door on it, going back to her perch on the couch. She did the same thing to Teresa the following day. She didn't care what they thought. If they had to be so pious in their thoughts about God and Billy, then God could have them all. They could all rot for all she cared.

She slept most of the day through the soap operas, waking up for a couple of hours before going to bed at night.

Rob's face took on a deep etched look. She thought his face might be sinking into itself. New lines, new caves.

On the seventh night, Rob held her unresponsive body and whispered, "I love you, Carolyn. I am scared for you. There is so much of life Billy gave. Just because he's gone doesn't mean he took it with him. There is still his memory to live for."

Something inside Carolyn snapped in place. Her mind lit up, the darkness slipping away. That night as she lay in bed, new, bright ideas burst like fireworks in her mind. She could take Billy with her still. She could envision him dancing and playing around her as she tried to reach the women before they made the fatal mistake. She would do it for Billy's sake, as always. Only now, she had more reason to fight. She would fight for the both of them, because Billy wasn't there to help.

·22·

Joann knew how Carolyn felt. Loss stripped one of all feeling. It made caring impossible. To care would be to hurt beyond all imagination.

No matter how much she understood Carolyn's feelings intellectually, in her heart she hurt when Carolyn slammed the door on her face and her love. Something inside wilted at the rejection of her support and concern she had brought with her.

She cried for the loss of Billy. She cried for the family. She even cried, again, for her own loss, for the holes that lay gaping in her own soul.

Teresa had told her she planned to take Carolyn and Rob a casserole. Joann shook her head. "Good luck," she replied. "I had my nose flattened by her door."

"It's worth a try. At least she'll know I care, even if she doesn't want it."

When Teresa received the same treatment Joann had, it hurt Teresa, too. "I must say," Teresa admitted, "that I didn't really think she'd slam the door in my face. I thought maybe you were too close to her, and she would accept me, a new friend."

Now, a week later, Joann had finally merged her intellect and emotions to accept Carolyn's actions.

She nursed Nicole in Teresa's living room while Vicki and Teresa worked in the kitchen on a birthday cake for Dan. The giggling filtered into the living room, until Joann couldn't stand to be left out anymore. She gathered up Nicole and went into the kitchen. "What are you guys laughing at?"

"Look at what Vicki made," Teresa said. Joann peered between them at the cake.

"Vicki did that?"

"You never did have much faith in me," Vicki pouted.

"It's terrific!" Joann said.

"It's perfect. Dan will die when he sees it."

"Why?" Vicki asked. "It makes sense for a postman to get a mailbag cake for his birthday."

"It's the letters sticking out of the bag, and who they are addressed to. How did you know the people on his route and what kind of mail they get?" Teresa asked her.

Vicki smiled. "There's nothing that gets by the 'ol slick Vick."

Joann nodded her approval. "Now if you can just apply that knowing to other areas of your life, like boys."

"Lay off Martin, would ya? I'm getting tired of your lectures."

Joann held her hand out as if for protection. "Don't get hostile. I'm only concerned about you."

"You sound like my mother."

Teresa answered the knock at the door. Her surprise drew them all to the door. "Carolyn!"

Joann reached the hallway just as Carolyn stepped in, again dressed to perfection. It looked like she had come from having her hair and nails done. "Hi," she said in her sweetest voice. "I came to apologize."

Teresa hugged her. "You don't need to apologize. We knew you only reacted out of hurt, not anger at us."

Joann gave her a hug next. "I'm sorry, Carolyn. I can never know how this has hurt you."

Carolyn wiped the tears from her eyes. "I'd say it's okay, but we'd all know that's a lie. I do hurt. I can't stand the thought of never seeing

Billy again." She breathed deeply, trying to hold the tears in. "I'll keep him alive by working harder."

She shook her head, motioning to the living room. "Can I come in?"

Teresa laughed. "Of course. I'm so glad to see you, I forgot my manners."

Vicki hung back, until the mood lightened. Then she said, "Hey, who are the presents for?"

Joann looked at her. "*Vicki!*"

"I'm just trying to get this show on the road. I love surprises, even when there's none for me."

Carolyn handed a large wrapped gift to Joann. "This is my apology for my rudeness. Will you forgive me?"

Joann's heart softened. "Of course I will." She handed Nicole to Vicki. Opening the package, she discovered four different country prints in shades of peach. "Carolyn. You didn't need . . ."

"There's enough to make a quilt. I got more of the dark one, so you could use it for the backing too." She turned to Teresa. "I was rude to you too. Will you forgive me?"

"Yes, what are friends for if we can't forgive each other." Teresa took the small gift Carolyn offered her. Inside were a pair of cloisonné earrings and a matching butterfly comb and bracelet.

Teresa's eyes lit up as she tried them on. "I tried to find something that would complement your dark skin," Carolyn told her. "There is nothing more beautiful than a woman in the proper accessories."

"You should know," Teresa said kindly.

"I hate to leave so soon, but I have a meeting I must go to. Ten days is much too long to be out of touch from my work."

An hour later Vicki left to meet Martin at the park, and Teresa and Joann stayed at the kitchen table for a cup of coffee. Joann did not want to be alone on this day and hoped Teresa didn't think of her as a nuisance. *How rude I can be?* Joann thought. *Teresa's only day to herself, and I take it away by sitting like a lump at her table.*

Teresa reached her hand out, touching Joann's arm. "What makes you so sad?"

Joann started from her reverie. "What?"

"I look at you, and I see so much sadness in your eyes. Where does it come from?"

Joann looked away, feeling stripped. "There's no sadness."

"Today, there is more than usual. Why?"

Joann's tears rose, ready to give her secret away. *This is the day.*

Seven years ago I had an abortion. And every year, on this day, I cry. "I'm fine. Must be my period or something."

Joann busied herself with Nicole, to avoid looking at Teresa.

Teresa stood up and washed her coffee mug out in the sink. "I know you're lying. But I'm always here, Joann, if you ever change your mind."

Joann nodded. "Thanks," she whispered.

* * *

The next night, Joann held Nicole's hot, limp body in her arms. Joann wished she could let Nicole know how much she loved her. She wanted to pray for her. But she could only be silent and hold her, stroking Nicole's soft, short hair.

How could I have done it? she thought. *My own little one. Gone.* Her chest ached with unshed tears. When they came, they were slow, gentle, yet persistent. Like her thoughts. *What kind of angel did I destroy?* She closed her eyes to visions of a child racing through the house, dirty hands gesturing as he shouted his intentions. A little girl skipped through, brunette ringlets dripping down her back. "I'm on my way to roller-skate with my friends," she said.

"Love you, Mom," they both shouted.

Joann held Nicole's head tighter to her chest. She had let one go. She had thought it would be okay.

Nicole's fevered breath came in tiny gasps. Joann feared for Nicole's life. She didn't trust what God would do. *I'm always looking for punishment around the next corner. As if the miscarriage wasn't punishment enough.*

Joann's tears left a damp spot on Nicole's hair. David came wandering out from the bedroom in a sleepy stagger. "Aren't you going to come to bed?"

"No," Joann whispered. "I don't want to leave her alone."

"The doctor said she'd be fine. It's only the flu."

"I know, but I don't trust him. Look at her, she's so limp, and I'm so scared."

David came over and put his arm around her, kissing Nicole's hot forehead. "Do you want me to sit up with you?"

Joann looked at her husband, seeing compassion she hadn't noticed in a long time. She reached a hand up to stroke his hair. "Thanks. You don't need to."

He nodded, kissed her on the cheek, and staggered away. A few moments later, he returned carrying his pillow and dragging a blanket, looking very much like a little boy visiting Grandma's.

He put the pillow on the couch, flopped his body on it, and pulled the blanket up to his chin. Joann almost smiled. "Do you ever get scared we'll lose Nicole, David?"

"Yes I do. But I'm more afraid of losing you."

"What do you mean?"

"Never mind, I shouldn't talk about it now."

"Go ahead."

He closed his eyes, and for a minute, Joann thought he had gone to sleep. "I don't feel like you are around for me anymore, Joann. You have time to care for the world, but never for me."

"You don't need caring for. You're an adult," she said gently.

"Aren't we partners? Aren't we supposed to share feelings, ideas, goals, hurts, and happiness?"

"Of course, and we do."

"Think about it, Joann, do we?"

Joann rocked and rocked, stroking Nicole's head, kissing it every so often. She forgot David asked her a question, being so preoccupied in fearing for Nicole. Then she looked at him in the darkness, almost surprised to see him.

"Joann, do we share?" he asked again.

She blushed, thankful David couldn't see it in the dark. She had been so involved in Nicole—again. "I think so," she said, pronouncing each word separately.

"When was the last time you asked me about work?"

"Yesterday."

"No, I mean work in a specific sense, not just 'How did work go today?' "

"I don't know."

"And when was the last time you shared your goals with me? When did you hear my hurts?"

"What hurts?"

"See? You don't even know."

Nicole began to whimper, so Joann put her on the breast. Her hot mouth made feeble attempts to suck.

"David, I. . . ." She wanted to say she was sorry, but that sounded too trite. It *was* too trite. Little thoughts flooded her. The times David came in, looking upset, tired, and all she did was glow about Nicole. The times when she did not greet him at the door, the times she spent

cooking for a poor family, then served him a TV dinner. She had justified it all at the time, telling herself David didn't really mind. Besides,
as long as he had a job, why discuss it?

"What am I doing to us, David?"

His voice came softly from the couch. "I don't know. It's killing me,
and what I feel for you. I planned never again to share my feelings with
you, but I guess in the middle of the night, plans change."

"David, I'll try. It's just that I . . . oh, I don't know. Nicole satisfies a
distant ache inside of me. So I concentrate on feeling happy, rather
than working on us. Maybe I've thought everything between us is so
perfect, I don't have to think about you."

"But you shut me out, Joann. I'm tired of being a single person in
this house. I thought we were supposed to be a family. Why do you
think I've been spending so much time away lately?"

Joann hung her head. "I hadn't noticed."

"See what I mean? I'm not even missed when I'm gone." David put
his arm across his eyes. "Do you realize what I feel like? A baby machine. I was only good for one thing. Now that I've fulfilled my 'duty,'
I'm tossed into the garbage."

Joann's mouth dropped open. David's quavering voice surprised her.
The only other time she'd seen David cry was when Nicole was born.

She got up from the rocker, and laid Nicole on a blanket on the floor.
She went to the couch and lay down next to David, her arms around
him. "I'm so sorry, David. I do love you." She stroked his hair. "I'll try
to change. Tell me about work now."

David shook his head, his voice coming out in a whisper.

"No. I'd feel childish. Maybe tomorrow, okay?"

"Okay."

"You'd better take care of Nicole. She needs you right now."

"So do you."

He smiled. "I always need you." He took his arm away from his eyes.
Joann pretended not to notice the tears in them.

·23·

 February tricked everyone into believing spring had come. Even the pear trees blossomed and the dogs began to shed. Then March roared in, the bully wind muscling his way around, blowing away all thought of spring. Joann didn't care. She loved it all. Even the permanent sadness that hung in her heart couldn't take away the joy that the end of winter brought. She worked diligently on the master quilt and the new wall hanging she intended to enter in the county fair only six months away.

Carolyn and Teresa promised to take her to lunch for her birthday in a week—without Nicole. As much as she loved feeling special on her birthday, Joann hated the thought of leaving Nicole with anyone. Even in church Nicole stayed with Joann instead of going into the nursery.

David encouraged her to go. "It will help *us*, Joann," he had told her. "You need to learn to let go of Nicole a little bit."

"But no one can care for her like her mother," Joann protested.

David held her in a bear hug. "You're right, no one can care for her like you. But a few hours away won't hurt her one bit. She loves Vicki, and probably won't even notice you are gone."

Joann reluctantly complied, and worried a bit about the whole agreement. She knew she needed to let go for David.

She worried, too, about Vicki. She seemed to be dragging the last couple of weeks. Her hair lost a bit of its luster, and Vicki turned down the chance to make chocolate-chip cookies. "The smell gags me," she had said.

Vicki told Joann her midterms wiped her out, but Joann blamed it on the time Vicki spent with Martin. The more times Joann saw him, the more she believed he had the charm of a poisonous viper. He knew what to say and when to say it. A nice guy. But something underneath the coolness made Joann wary. Maybe it was the way he told Vicki what to do and she did it.

I did that with whoever I was dating. Especially Ross. Aren't we supposed to be submissive?

But Vicki wouldn't let Joann talk about him anymore. She met all questions with silence. So Joann stopped trying. Instead, she looked forward to her birthday celebration.

* * *

Teresa gave the lemon a quick twist over the water glass. With a dainty move, it landed in the glass, pushing the ice aside. She picked up the forest green linen napkin, dabbing the two stray drops of lemon juice from her fingers. "Well, ladies, we've come to celebrate. . . ."

"Ladies?" Joann quipped, her lemon spraying drops on everyone. "Since when did we change from girls?"

"Hmmm," Carolyn murmured. "Newspapers claim we are women once we hit twenty."

"Don't you hate watching 'Miss America' anymore? All the contestants are younger than we are," Joann pouted.

"Ain't that the awful truth," Carolyn shook her head as she looked at the menu. "But they look older."

"Don't I get to finish my sentence?" Teresa asked.

"No," Joann and Carolyn said in unison.

Everyone laughed. "Friends are terrific," Joann said. "I want to talk."

"You always do," Carolyn teased.

Joann would have stuck her tongue out at her, but she was supposed to be a mature woman now.

"So go ahead, since you won't let me talk," encouraged Teresa.

"It makes me feel so good that you would think of me like this."

"Like how?" asked Teresa.

"Like special. It's nice of you to take me to lunch for my birthday."

Carolyn looked at Teresa. "Who said anything about taking her to lunch?"

Teresa shrugged. "Not me, certainly. I thought *she* was taking *us* to lunch."

They both nodded and turned to look at Joann, who laughed. "I mean it. David is a sweetie, but he doesn't know how important it is for me to do something *on* my birthday. Not the weekend after."

"Men don't know the first thing about birthdays," Carolyn agreed.

"What do you mean? Dan always does something great for mine. Why last year . . ."

Carolyn and Joann moaned. They were tired of hearing all the wonderful things Dan did for Teresa. It didn't seem fair that one of their little group had a perfect husband. She knew it too, and loved making them jealous whenever she could.

"Ready to order?" the waitress asked.

"No," they said in unison.

"Okay, I'll be back."

"What are you getting?" Joann asked Teresa.

"Order whatever you want," Carolyn said before Teresa answered.

Joann laughed. Carolyn knew her well. "Is there any Parmesan cheese in the onion soup?"

"You and your allergies," Teresa muttered. "What a pain."

"What, me or the allergies?"

"Both."

"Thanks."

"You're welcome."

"Don't you two ever look at each other when you're talking?" Carolyn asked.

"Only when there's nothing better to look at," Teresa said without ever lifting her head from the menu.

Joann couldn't ask for a better place to have a birthday lunch. The restaurant consisted of elegant refurbished train cars that had transported the rich and well-to-do during the 1920s. The walls of the car they sat in were paneled warm walnut, with inlaid scroll designs done in blond birch tones. In the corner of the room stood a brass washbasin, with a beveled mirror hanging above it. The friends sat in their own compartment with the door closed. The waitress knocked to enter. She carried their lunch, croissants stuffed with shrimp, cheese, and avocado.

"I'll have to bring David here for our anniversary," Joann said between bites.

Carolyn and Teresa nodded, their mouths too busy to speak.

As they waited for after-meal coffee, Carolyn pulled her purse up to the table. "Oh, Teresa, I almost forgot. I got this new booklet in the mail yesterday. You'll love it. I think I'm going to order a couple hundred to start."

"Hmm. Let me see." Teresa dabbed her mouth with the napkin, reaching across the table for the booklet. As she thumbed through it, her eyes lit up. "Oh, yes. Yes. Oh, this one's real good. Where'd you get this?"

"From some new organization in the Midwest."

Joann felt her joy slipping away. Her stomach tightened. *I'm going to be sick. I'm stuck. I shouldn't have slipped into this booth first. That's what I get for being selfish in choosing the window seat.*

Now what? How do I get myself out of this one?

"Here, Joann, want to take a look?" Carolyn laid a booklet in front of her.

"Not yet. I'm afraid mother nature is calling."

"You can wait a sec, Joann. I don't know why you want to avoid the subject all the time."

"It's just that I don't want to talk about it on my birthday, okay?"

"You never want to talk about it."

Teresa, in her merciful way, turned the conversation away from Joann. "How long do you think it will take to get more of these?"

"Oh, a couple of weeks, at least. I wanted to get them before the next rally."

"When's that?"

"Two weeks from Saturday."

"Is that the one in Santa Rosa?"

"Uh-huh. It's going to last all day—with guest speakers and the whole bit."

"Will you go, Joann?" Teresa asked.

"Of course not," Carolyn snipped. "Joann will never come."

"Yes I will," Joann lied in defense. "What's the date of the next one?"

"I said two weeks from Saturday. That would be the twenty-sixth."

"Too bad," Joann answered, hoping they couldn't detect her shaking hands. "That's David's only Saturday off this month. We've promised we won't plan anything separate on that day."

"Could you both come?" Carolyn asked.

Joann forced a smile. "David doesn't like things like that."

"Neither do you," Carolyn added.

Teresa rerouted the conversation again. "Carolyn, where do you think they got these terrific pictures?"

"They are great, aren't they? You'd think the clinics wouldn't allow such incriminating pictures to be taken. It's not good for business, I wouldn't think, to show all those body pieces in a bloody, mangled mess."

Joann's stomach pushed its way up, as she tried to think of spring, wild flowers, the lake, anything else.

"No, those aren't the ones I'm talking about," Teresa said. "I don't like those. I think we could do without them. The better pictures, I think, are the positive ones."

"Positive ones?"

"Like these." Teresa held up the booklet, showing a tiny little baby inside its amniotic sac. The fingers that held it were huge in comparison. Such a tiny little thing, and yet it looked perfect.

Teresa continued. "I think a positive approach is better. Show people what their baby looks like, and I bet they would give their choice more consideration. I also think a great many of them would choose life."

Joann tried not to look, but the tiny child drew her eyes. "How . . . old . . . is . . . it?" she asked.

"Let me see . . . eleven weeks."

She closed her eyes, and her heart dropped. *That could be your baby, Joann. It's the same age your baby was. Look what you've done.* "Excuse me, Carolyn. A second's up. I've really got to go to the rest room."

She ruined her makeup with the cold water she splashed on her face. She panted like a dog to keep from losing lunch. *At least you have a birthday to celebrate,* her mind taunted. *Some people never get a chance to have their first one.*

Joann pounded the tile. She wanted to cry, but her tears stuck. She wanted to scream, to throw up. But she couldn't do any of it. Just like she couldn't change the past.

She waited until she controlled her emotions before returning to the table. Relieved, she saw the pamphlets had disappeared.

Teresa looked at her with concern. "Are you okay? You don't look so well."

"I think there was Parmesan in the soup. Someday I'll learn to avoid onion soup unless I make it."

Five waitresses flooded the little room, one carrying a large piece of mud pie with a candle in it. "Happy birthday to you. . . ." Everyone sang. Each of the other waitresses carried a helium balloon. Joann felt the color return to her face, and the joy to her heart. The three women shared the huge piece of rich pie. When stuffed, each let out a sigh of fullness. Carolyn squirmed around in her seat a moment, her lips pulling tight. She rubbed the handle of her purse. She turned in her seat to face Joann. "Don't you have anything that consumes you, that forces you to fight for what is right?"

Her tone, accusing Joann of slothfulness, got to Joann. "We all have our consuming passions, Carolyn. Ours just happen to be different." Joann could not disguise the tension in her voice. She tried to remain civil and polite.

A haughty, self-righteous look covered Carolyn's face. "Yes, but quilting doesn't help anyone."

"In your opinion," Joann replied, not quite believing herself. "I make the mothers of babies happy. When people look at what I have created, hanging on their walls, they feel nice; when I teach them how to quilt, it makes them feel good about themselves and that their time is being spent wisely. God gave me a gift. He gave you a gift. Just because they're different doesn't mean one is less important."

"Big deal. You aren't saving lives. You don't even care about saving lives. . . ."

"Not everyone can save lives, Carolyn," Teresa interjected softly. "Some have to maintain the lives that are already here. Don't you think we are all called to different tasks?"

"Yes and no. I think all are called against the horrors of the world."

"Carolyn," Teresa said gently. "Your anger and zeal are driving people away. That approach doesn't help. I see you lack the compassion you scream at the abortionists to have. You have lost compassion for the hurting women in zeal for the baby."

"Well, they have an awful lot of compassion for the woman and none for the baby."

"Agreed. But don't you think there has to be a middle ground somewhere? A compassion for both? An understanding of the adult who is here, so that *she* can understand the child that is growing and maturing inside her?"

Joann grabbed those statements, locking them inside for safekeeping.

Compassion for both. What if someone had known, had compassion for me and my baby? Would I have made another choice?

"No one understands, do they?" Carolyn shouted as she stood up and threw her napkin on the table. She pulled out her purse and threw down a twenty-dollar bill. "That should cover my part of the bill. I'll see you two later." The door slammed behind her.

Tears filled Joann's eyes. "Some birthday celebration."

"I'm sorry it turned out this way," Teresa told her.

Joann's eyes flashed with fire. "Since when did you get involved in Carolyn's abortion crusade?"

"I've always been interested in doing something about abortion."

"You're going to be like her?"

"I don't plan to. I'm interested in their literature and approach, but only from an analysis standpoint. I'm not sure which direction I want to go. I've been praying a lot about it, but don't have any direction yet."

Joann calmed down. "I'm sorry I yelled at you."

"I understand."

·24·

•• Vicki looked sloppier and more wrinkled than usual. She didn't even jump when Nicole cried. She seemed weary and listless with a faraway look in her eyes. Joann felt a pang of something move within her—a tinge of undefined pain.

"You aren't concentrating, Vicki," Joann said softly.

"Sorry." Vicki poked another hole into her appliqué, letting the needle sit there, half in and half out.

"Is something bothering you?"

Big tears rolled down Vicki's face, dropping onto her appliqué. She stared at her needle, without moving.

Joann put her work down, and put her hand on Vicki's. "Can I help?"

Shoulders shrugged, tears flowed faster. Vicki picked the needle out, and began random pokes into the fabric, over and over, without speaking. Joann got up and returned with a box of tissues. She pulled one out and handed it to Vicki. It sat ignored. The needle poked and poked. Nicole cried from her bed, and no one stood to get her. The needle stopped, and Vicki put her hands to her face. Nicole, not used to being ignored, screamed for attention. "I'll be right back," Joann whispered.

Joann ran to get Nicole, and changed her so fast, she stuck her finger with the diaper pin. She grabbed an extra diaper and blanket before returning to the living room. She pulled the rocking chair as close to Vicki as she could. Settling down in it, she began to nurse Nicole. As she rocked, she noticed Vicki had stopped crying, but continued to tremble. "You can tell me anything, Vicki."

Vicki shook her head. "Not this," she said, barely audible.

"Is it about Martin?"

The tissue turned to shreds in Vicki's wringing hands.

Vicki breathed a deep sigh. "I'm pregnant."

The rocker stopped, and so did Joann's heart. It must have. Dead. Lead. Stopped. Then it started to race. Ross. "*Ross, I'm pregnant.*" Joann cried. She stood up, still nursing Nicole, and hugged Vicki. Both of them cried until Nicole was full.

Nicole bounced on Joann's shoulder, as Joann walked her around the room, instinct controlling her, telling her Nicole must be burped. "What are you going to do, Vicki? What happened?"

"I went out to dinner with Martin. We went to his bedroom afterward to listen to records like we always do. But this time he pushed me into a corner. He made me. I didn't want to, really, Joann."

"Rape? He raped you?"

"Don't call it that. I just didn't want to."

"Then that's rape."

"But I love Martin. That makes it different."

"Does it?"

"Yeah. I might have someday. You know, when we got married or something."

"Do you still love him?"

"I don't know. I think so."

"Have you told him?"

"Yeah."

"What'd he say?"

"He said to get lost. Get an abortion."

Shivers went up Joann's spine. "*It's okay, Joann. We have to. It's the only way. No one will get hurt this way.*" "So what do you think?"

"I think he's right."

"Why?"

"I'm not old enough to have a baby. I didn't want to be pregnant. I didn't even ask to. . . ." Tears flowed down her face again.

"Have you told your parents?"

"Are you kidding? They'd kill me."

"Why?"

"First of all, they wouldn't believe Martin forced me. They don't trust me. Second, we can't afford for me to be pregnant. We can't afford to eat as it is. How would we pay for a doctor? I imagine it must cost a fortune."

"It does. But I think there must be agencies to help."

"I don't want anyone else to know. I know my parents will kick me out and never let me back in."

Unfortunately she's probably right, Joann thought. "So, do you want an abortion?"

"I guess so. I don't see any other way."

"Have you called the clinic?"

"No. I was hoping you'd help me."

"I will." She hugged Vicki as best she could with one arm. "You know I will."

The next day, Joann picked up a drooping Vicki after school and drove to a remote pay phone. "I don't want to have any Morristown numbers on our phone bill," she explained to Vicki. "David checks every number to make certain we aren't overcharged."

They made arrangements for the following Saturday, David's promised day off. "I'll save some breast milk and freeze it. David has offered to watch Nicole for the day if I ever want to go shopping. So that's what we'll tell him, okay?"

Vicki nodded obediently.

*   *   *

It's aggravating to have the weather not cooperate with a bad day, Joann thought as she packed her handwork and cursed the sun. She gave David terse instructions for Nicole.

"I thought this was supposed to be a day of shopping," David said. "You know, fun."

Joann forced a smile. "I'm sorry. Thanks for watching Nicole. I guess I'm just trying to get going, trying to push myself too hard."

Vicki looked pale and frightened. She slipped quietly into the car,

151

and sat with her hands folded in her lap like a small schoolchild. She stared straight ahead, saying nothing.

Joann didn't say anything either. The car wended its way through beautiful trees, hills, and lakes, their beauty unnoticed that day.

When the signs on the merging freeways told them they were almost there, Joann finally spoke. "Is this what you really want, Vicki?"

"I don't think I have any other choice, do you?"

"No, I don't think you do." Carolyn's stern face flashed in Joann's mind. What would Carolyn do if she knew? Images of Carolyn and Billy, Carolyn marching with angry signs, flashed across Joann's mind. *To hell with Carolyn. What does she know about pain and fear anyway? You make the best choices with what you have. How can she condemn that?*

Waves of fear rushed over Joann when she saw the brick building. She looked at Vicki, remembering her own fears, her own pain of so many years ago. Now maybe she could help someone else through it.

They silently walked together into the building. A kind receptionist took Vicki's name, her savings from baby-sitting, and a few dollars from Joann's secret stash. They sat in a room of stunned and frightened people. Rustling magazine pages and an occasional sniffle or whisper broke the silence. Vicki stared at a rubber plant, and Joann pulled her handwork from her bag. She felt like a mother taking her daughter to get help.

Am I really helping her?

Of course you are.

She forced her attention on her work. Each stitch, even and fine. "Put that away," Vicki hissed.

Joann looked confused. "Why?"

"It's for a baby."

Joann blushed. She hadn't thought about what she worked on. She stuffed it into the bag and pulled out a kitchen dish towel on which she planned to appliqué a frog family.

"Miss V.R., please."

Vicki jumped, and looked around the room, hoping they called someone else. She got up as slowly as she could and walked to the nurse. She turned to Joann, a pleading look in her eyes.

Joann watched the door close, and went back to work. Her concentration clogged as she remembered a song that haunted her quiet moods.

The night and I are much the same,
We both do play a hiding game.
Full of darkness, full of sin,
It could be said I'm night's own twin.
Each can cover what shouldn't be seen,
Evil hides in darkness' screen.

One day I turn around to see,
A teenage girl so much like me.
Her laughter, joy, mistakes she's made,
Her plans for digging with a spade.
Compassion flows from deep within.
Perhaps she too, will be night's twin.

Joann saw herself getting undressed, and lying on the short, slanted table. She felt the awkwardness and humiliation of the position they put her in, the pain of the injection, the dilation, the sound of suction, the pulling sensation. She shook her head. *She has no other choice. Just like me.*

She bent her head over her work, trying to see it. She remembered the juice and cookies afterward. Hawaiian Punch and Fig Newtons. She couldn't eat those anymore. It made her sick to look at them. Looking around the recovery room, she had felt the shame they all shared. The humiliation. The loss. *It was the best choice, the only choice you had, Joann.*

Joann noticed that tears spotted her appliqué. Her insides wrenched and tugged.

"*Ross, we've killed our baby.*"

"*Honey, don't worry, we'll have another.*"

We killed not only our baby, but something inside of us.

Joann couldn't stop the feelings now if she wanted. They poured over her, tormented her, swept her away. Each moment of pain, each moment of sadness, each night of dreams filled with fear and waking in a sweat. The secrets, the tears, the second baby, lost by miscarriage. The years of sadness and loss, never to be filled again.

Joann stuffed her work back into the bag, rushing to the receptionist. "I've got to talk to Vicki, I mean, V.R., right away please."

"I think she's in surgery now."

"Please go check, *please.* I just need to talk to her."

The receptionist smiled and left her desk. She returned in a moment. "She's next, but we'll take another in before her. Come on back."

Looking like a frightened child, Vicki sat in a folding chair, her hospital gown draped around her, her clothes in a bag at her feet. As she gazed at Joann, her eyes looked dead.

"Vicki, listen to me. I don't think you should go through with this, at least not today."

Vicki stopped fingering her gown. Joann went on. "I think maybe we could think of another alternative, okay? We'll ask around at all the agencies. I'll go with you to tell your parents. You can live with David and me. Anything, but don't do this, okay? At least not today?"

Vicki's voice matched the deadness in her eyes. "Why, Joann? I thought this was my only choice."

"Do you *really* want to do this, Vicki? Because if you do, I'll shut up and never say another word."

Vicki shook her head. "I don't know, Joann. I'm so confused. I *don't* want to, but I don't see that there's any other way."

"I don't either. But maybe God will help us think of something."

Vicki stared at her, then picked up her bag, and disappeared into a cubicle. She emerged, looking confused.

The receptionist refunded the money. "If you change your mind, you give me a call, okay?"

"You don't mind refunding the money?" Joann asked, surprised.

"This happens at least once a week. Pre-op jitters. Most people are back in a week."

"We won't be."

The woman smiled smugly. "Oh."

The drive home was like a sigh of relief. "Why did you come barging in like that?" Vicki asked her.

Joann drove awhile without saying anything. She parked off the side of the road on the western end of Silver Lakes. She motioned for Vicki to get out of the car. They sat on the edge of the lake.

"So why'd you stop me?" Vicki asked again.

"I've never told anyone this, Vicki." She drew her finger in the soft dirt. "I had an abortion."

"When?" Vicki asked in disbelief.

"My second year of college. I didn't have any other choice."

"So why not me? You've survived okay."

"I haven't though. I have nightmares every week. I relive the abortion. I see babies waving at me. I hurt when I hold Nicole. There is a profound sadness I can't explain. And I never really put the sadness together with the abortion until today. Some of the other stuff, sure. I guess I've believed the nightmares were God's punishment. I've never gotten over it, Vicki. And it's been seven years. I made the only choice I could have made, and it was a terrible choice."

"Do you think it was a wrong choice?"

"No and yes. I made the wrong choice when I went to bed with Ross. It was irresponsible, stupid, and wrong. The only problem with the abortion is that I haven't been able to shake the feeling of loss, of grief."

"But the abortion itself wasn't wrong?"

"I don't know, Vicki. One day I know I made the best choice, and the next, I wonder what my six-year-old would be doing, or who she would look like."

"So what am *I* going to do, Joann?"

"I don't know, but we'll think of something." She ran her fingers through her hair, looking at the ground, wishing the dirt had the answer. "We'll think of all the options, but at the end of it all, Vicki, it's got to be your decision. I'll be with you no matter what."

They brushed the dirt off their pants, and climbed back into the car.

·25·

"·Back so soon?" David asked. "Usually when you go to Morristown I'm lucky if you're home in time for dinner." He smiled, getting up to kiss Joann on the cheek.

Vicki hung her head. "I'm going to see Nicole." Her voice, soft with shame, touched David.

He watched her disappear into the bedroom. "Where'd you go? What happened?"

Joann dropped her purse and keys on the kitchen table. The old wooden chair creaked as she sat in it. "To Morristown."

"What'd you buy?"

"Nothing."

"You mean to tell me you couldn't find one pair of baby socks in all of Morristown?"

Joann turned her head away. David knew when she lied. "I forgot about the socks." *That's true, isn't it?*

David reached across the table and grabbed her wrist. His voice softened to a whisper. "What's wrong with Vicki?"

"I'll tell you later." Joann hoped he would forget her promise.

The elephant didn't forget. Vicki had finally gone home after dinner, sent off with hugs and promises, when he asked again. "What's wrong with Vicki?"

Joann slid a diaper pin through layers of double diapers. Stuffing the whole mess inside plastic pants, she tried to put off the answer again. "Let me put Nicole down first."

"*Now,* Joann."

Little toes wiggled inside woolly pj feet. Little thumbs got caught in the sleeves, and had to be released from their prison. "I promised not to tell."

David leaned forward, shoving his hands through his hair in frustration. "Stop playing your stupid games, Joann."

"I'm not playing games, David. I don't know if I should break a confidence."

"Fine. Just don't expect me to baby-sit anymore for an unknown jaunt of yours."

"Don't you trust me, David?"

"Yes, but you obviously don't trust me."

Joann picked up Nicole, and sat in the rocker with her. She brushed her wispy baby hair with her fingers. Each rock brought her tears closer to the surface. "Oh, David," she whispered. "I love you."

His eyes met Joann's, pleading together with his voice. "Then trust me."

Joann kissed Nicole's head, then lay her cheek on it, smelling the sweet, soft, baby smell. Her heart ached. *My babies. Two that I will never rock.*

Joann carried Nicole to bed. Nicole smiled sleepily when she saw all the yellow and brown bears cavorting on sheet, quilt, and bumper pads. *Everything perfect for a perfect baby.* Nicole's plump thumb easily found its niche. As Joann covered her with the sheet, she stroked her head. "I love you, my little Nicole."

Night-light on, overhead light off, the room looked serene and safe. "Like a womb," Joann said, then shuddered.

She turned down the light next to David before sitting on the couch. He looked expectantly at her.

"Vicki's pregnant."

David dropped his head into his hands. After a moment, he spoke. "What's she going to do about it?"

"She's not going to get an abortion."

"That goes without saying, doesn't it?"

"We went to Morristown today for her to get an abortion."

David's face took on a look of total incomprehension. "*Why?*"

"It seemed to be the only answer."

"Why?"

"Martin forced her. Her parents can't afford the doctor bills. They would probably kick her out, too. It seemed to be the best and only choice."

"Abortion is never the best choice."

Joann shuddered. "How can you be so sure?"

"Just because someone is pregnant at the wrong time, or out of place, or it will cause great heartache, doesn't mean it is right to destroy that little life."

"But the woman's life, isn't that destroyed by an unwanted pregnancy?"

David looked thoughtful. "I think that's temporary, but abortion is permanent."

"I don't understand how the unwanted pregnancy is temporary. You've always got the child."

"That's just it. The humiliation or stress of having a baby at the wrong time is immense for a while. But when that child comes, so much of your opinion is changed."

"Spoken like a true man, the one who does not have to care for the child."

"Neither does the mother. There are so many wonderful parents like Carolyn, waiting to have a child. I don't think it's right to deny a child life because it's inconvenient for the mother."

Inconvenient. The word struck Joann like a fist. *Why not add* selfish *to the list too?* "How did we get onto this subject, anyway?" Joann asked angrily.

"Because you and Vicki, for some stupid reason, thought that was the answer to her dilemma."

"Then what is?"

"I don't know. She can move in with us, give it up for adoption, keep it, I don't care. Just don't try to correct one tragedy with another."

"Isn't it a tragedy to have a pregnant sixteen-year-old?"

"Yes, that's the first tragedy. Don't destroy the baby and Vicki by getting an abortion."

"What makes you think Vicki would be destroyed?" Joann's voice was getting a bit arrogant.

"I've watched you," David said. Joann's heart fluttered in fear. "When you lost our first baby, it was as though you lost a child we had known. I don't think you can snatch a baby from its mother's womb and then say she doesn't suffer grief. And then for that woman to know she made the choice, not God or nature, or whatever she believes happens in a miscarriage, how can she not suffer?"

Joann stared at the wall. "Where do you get all this knowledge?"

"Like I said, I've watched you. And there's this gal at work. She was crying one day, and I asked her why. She said it was the anniversary of her abortion—nine years ago! I talked with her more about it, and she told me how it all still hurts. I can't think she's the only one. I don't care what anyone says. I watched you lose one that wasn't your fault. I couldn't imagine how you would react if you did it on purpose."

"I've got to do the dishes," Joann said, jumping from the couch.

With soapy water to her elbows, tears dropped from her face into the water. *It was okay, wasn't it God? I did the best I could, didn't I?* screamed her confused and tormented mind. David wrapped his arms around her waist and whispered in her ear. "I love you. I'm sorry I got angry. I couldn't understand why you would even consider abortion."

Joann leaned to the side, pulling the hand towel from the ring. David let go of her, and she dried her hands. "Let's sit on the couch."

She sat cross-legged, facing David.

"David, there's something I never told you."

"Yeah, babe, what is it?"

"It's something I did that's terrible."

"Ah c'mon, babe, you could never do anything *that* terrible."

Tears began to pour down her face. "Joann, I'm sorry, I didn't mean it like that." David pulled her close to him. She covered her face with her hands. "So what is it, babe?"

"It was before I ever met you," Joann pleaded.

"We all did stuff we're sorry for, Jo." David sounded scared.

"I had . . . an . . ." Joann spoke between sobs. "David, I had an abortion."

David stopped stroking Joann's hair. His hand dropped to the couch. *Silence can hurt so bad sometimes.*

David grabbed one of Joann's hands, squeezed it, then walked out the front door.

·26·

J oann's tears stopped in stunned silence. She stared at the door, hoping it would reopen. She heard the car start, then race off. David only did that when mad—real mad. Her hands twisted and pulled at each other. Her feet tapped, her mouth twitched. *Why did I have to tell him? Stupid fool. Are you trying to lose everyone you ever loved? Just kill them all off, why don't you?*

She went back to washing the dishes. Soap bubbles and water splashed everywhere. When she finished the dishes, she scrubbed the oven, then the refrigerator. She vacuumed dust from underneath the refrigerator. She cleaned the grease from the top of it too. She wiped each shelf and cupboard clean. She swept and mopped the kitchen floor. At midnight she vacuumed the floors, dusting each piece of furniture down to the rungs of the kitchen chairs.

The bathroom came next, every inch scrubbed clean. With nothing left to clean in the whole house, Joann sat down and cried from exhaustion and fear. Her bones shook, her body screamed for rest. And still, no thoughts would come. Nothing of comfort. Nothing of anything.

Tiptoeing into Nicole's room she peeked in the bed and put her hand on Nicole's back, feeling the rhythm of her breathing. At least there was Nicole. Teddy called to her from the corner. He found his way into her arms, but something lacked in his comfort this time. It wasn't the same. He couldn't help.

With a hug, Joann set him back in his corner, and went back to Nicole. She picked her up and cradled her, smelling her soft head. The rocking chair welcomed them, and they rocked and rocked in the comfort of each other's arms. At three in the morning, exhaustion won the battle for Joann's attention. She returned Nicole to her bed.

Joann dragged her pillow and blanket from the cold and empty double bed to the couch. In spite of her fear and sorrow, she fell right to sleep.

✳   ✳   ✳

The awful reminder that David had left hit the minute Joann woke and realized she slept on the couch. The heaviness inside took all joy from seeing Nicole. Nicole's arms reached up to her momma, her tears begging for her to be changed and fed breakfast. Joann did all her tasks without her usual satisfaction. *Oh God, please bring David back.* The words spun around in her mind, driving her crazy.

She set Nicole's infant seat on the kitchen table and tied a bib around her neck. She mixed warm formula with the rice cereal and took a tiny spoon from a drawer. Nicole's arms and legs flapped with excitement.

The front door opened, closed. A spoonful of cereal stopped in midair. "David?"

David, his hair and clothes disheveled, peeked into the kitchen. Joann's gaze locked with his, both afraid to show any emotion. Joann stood, dropping the spoon back into the bowl.

David came to her, and hugged her. "I love you," he said.

"How can you?" Joann asked.

"I don't hate you for what you did, if that's what you think."

"Of course I think that. After all the things that you said about abortion and how stupid. . . ."

"That's what I had to go think over. I had to see why anyone would be so stupid. I sat in the park all night, thinking about it all. I remembered some of the things you said, like having no other choice, and fear,

161

and so on. I will never really understand because I've never been there.

"When I was a kid, I threw a match on a dry grassy hill by our home. I didn't think much about it, I just wondered what it would look like, or if it would really catch on fire. That whole hill went up in flames in a matter of minutes, destroying one house. Out of fear, I pulled the fire alarm box and ran. I ran for two miles to a grocery store and stayed there until I thought it safe to go home. Out of fear, I never told anyone. I was so afraid I'd be caught.

"I guess because of that, I can understand how fear will drive you to make decisions you would never make when not afraid. But abortion, Joann. *Abortion?*"

"I couldn't have that baby, David. It would have destroyed too many people."

David shook his head. "I don't understand. Tell me about it."

"I already did."

"No, I want to know everything. How and where you met this guy . . . everything."

"David, don't you think it will only hurt you?"

"Yes, but I want to know, I want to understand. I don't think I can unless you tell me the whole story."

Joann sat down to feed Nicole. Having something to do might make it easier as she tried to explain.

"I met Ross my first semester at college."

"I thought you said you went to that exclusive Christian college."

"I did. The students and faculty alike were all carefully scrutinized, checked and rechecked, for devotion to God. They demanded strict adherence to the Bible. A violation of God's law brought swift punishment.

"Everyone felt happy, safe, and at ease. Defenses weren't necessary to maintain faith. The very environment seemed protected from sin. The administration did not allow sin, so there was true freedom there."

David rolled his eyes. "No one can stop sin."

Joann sighed in aggravation. "I loved that school. I could be myself for the first time, without worrying about being a good witness to my friends. And then I met Ross. He was my psychology professor."

"Your *professor?* Oh, Joann . . . ," David shook his head.

"David, don't make it sound so sordid and evil."

"Wasn't it, Joann?"

Joann's insides quaked at his anger. She caught the oozing cereal from Nicole's mouth and shoved it back in. "Look, David, I told you I didn't think you'd want to hear what happened."

"Maybe I don't, but tell me anyway."

"I was attracted to him. He didn't speak to me, except as prof to student, until the beginning of my sophomore year." She watched David pace the kitchen floor, cracking his knuckles.

"After a while we fell in love, and well . . ."

"Say it, Joann, you went to bed with him."

"I . . . we . . . uh . . . yeah. David, we don't have to get into details."

David leaned on the kitchen counter, staring out the window. "How many times, Joann?"

"How many times, what?"

"How many times did you go to bed with him?"

"That isn't relevant. The point is, I got pregnant. I couldn't keep my mind on class at all that morning I got the test results back. After class, I went to Ross's desk and blurted it out."

She washed Nicole's face and took her from the infant seat. She started shaking.

"After I told him, Ross got the name of an abortion clinic. He even got me an appointment. When he told me that, I stared at him, unbelieving. For some crazy reason, I had expected him to propose. Or to have an answer. I started crying. We talked about it for a while, and I realized I had no other choice but abortion. If I remained pregnant, I would be kicked out of school and Ross too."

"He *should* have been kicked out."

"What kind of place would Ross have in this world if he couldn't teach in a Christian college? How could he reach his dream of becoming head of the psychology department?

"And me, my ambitions, my desires, my dreams. What would become of them with a child hanging on my dress? And what about my future ministry? What Christian organization would accept a woman who, as a Christian, got pregnant with an illegitimate child? What about the friends I had so carefully spoken to and 'planted seeds' for their salvation?

"Then I thought about my parents. My parents would die. They would not understand. They taught me to play the game they did. To put on a Christian face no matter what's taking place at home."

David looked at her, incredulous. "They would have understood."

"Now I know they could have lived through it, but back then I was sure they could never understand. They would have been furious with me for ruining their reputation. Ross and I talked about the abortion, and I remember him saying that we had no other choice. He had thought of all the other options; there just weren't any that could work. He was crying."

David sneered. "What a jerk. I can't believe how he got what he wanted, using you in the process." David jumped down from the counter, walking away from her. "The whole thing makes me sick, Joann. You and him and the whole mess. I'm going to work."

Joann followed him into the bedroom. "You don't have to be there for two more hours."

"I'm not staying here, that's for sure."

Joann was still dressing Nicole when she heard the door slam. She dressed herself, then put Nicole in the stroller. "We're going for a walk, my little precious one. Mommy has to think."

As Joann walked along the lakeshore, she paid no attention to the scenery. The stroller wheels clattered over the rough street, joggling her thoughts. She thought back to how it all began. The scene rolled through her mind, like watching an old, sad movie.

The first day in psychology class, she knew there was something special about Ross. He couldn't have been much older than she was, she decided. Later she discovered he was eight years older.

He was gorgeous! Blond hair, blond mustache, blue eyes, the color of the ocean surrounding the islands of paradise.

She tried to ignore *him* and listen to his words as a teacher, but she could swear his eyes were on her, too.

After class, she had to get a closer look, so she went to him and said something stupid like, "It's going to be a good class. I'm glad you're the professor." She could have sworn he smiled and said, "Me too," but she had already fled out the door.

After finals she realized her imaginings were not imaginings at all. Her roommate told her, "Joann, I can't believe how the sparks fly between you two," one night at bedtime.

"Oh, get off it, Becky. It's all my problem. A stupid crush I can't seem to shake."

"Do you want to shake it?"

"Yes and no. I know it's not proper to long for a teacher, but I can't seem to help it."

She didn't really want to shake it. It was such a wonderful, awful, feeling. Bittersweet. She wanted him!

Becky went on. "Well you could probably have him for the asking. It's so obvious, I don't know why you haven't noticed it before."

The next quarter and the next, she signed up for his classes. She hated herself for wanting him, but part of her always hoped he'd notice.

During the summer, she thought she'd never stop thinking about him. The first day of fall classes, she felt a difference about him that she couldn't figure out. This time, it became obvious he avoided her. He never looked at her once during the first class. One minute before class ended, he consulted his roll book and said, "Joann Miller, please see me after class."

She wondered what she had done wrong. She stayed in her seat until all the other students left. The door closed. Ross, still consulting papers in front of him, said, "Come into my office, please."

His office was a corner of the classroom, blocked off by partitions and a door that locked. She stepped inside, he closed it, turned to her, and smiled with such warmth, she felt hugged.

"Joann, I hoped you would come back."

"You did?"

"All summer, I could only see one face. Yours. I couldn't get you out of my mind. You're a special woman."

Suddenly he seemed awkward. "I had to tell you that. You can go now."

She felt funny. Dismissed, but not dismissed. She didn't want to leave. She wanted some excuse to stay, so she started blabbing. "I'm very interested in psychology. Maybe in becoming a psychologist. Are there any special things I should know about, study, or classes to take?" She hoped he didn't see through the lie.

He thought for a moment. "I'll make up some lists, think about it some. See me after class on Wednesday."

"Okay."

Every class day after that, she waited behind to do a little extra studying with Ross. Sometimes other students were there, sometimes not. When other students stayed, Ross played cool. When they were alone, less studying got done. They talked most of the time as they shared their lives.

The stroller stuck on a large rock. "I should be paying attention to where I'm going, instead of daydreaming. Right, Nicole? But the daydreaming makes me remember the wonderful, good feelings I had back then. Oh, I wish you could understand."

She knew the college rules stated a prof may not date a student. But they were not dating. They were friends. And then it grew.

The first time he kissed her, he looked surprised and a bit ashamed. She never wanted it to end. Just a kiss. That's all she wanted. Forever.

After that, they had to break rules. How could they deny what was right because of a simple rule? They had dinner. Then another and another. Then one night it happened. It wasn't planned. It wasn't planned against, either. For the first time in her life, she wanted what she shouldn't have, and didn't care about the consequences . . . but the consequences came all too soon.

After vomiting for the third morning in a row, she knew. She didn't need a test to tell her the obvious. But she felt she needed something more concrete to base her knowledge on before she could tell Ross. So she had the blood test, then came to class. She hated telling him like that.

Joann shivered as she remembered. *That night was the worst night of my life.* After he broke the news to her about the abortion, she started crying. He held her close and she could feel the tears streaming down his face. "I can't marry you, Joann. Not now. I would lose my job. Jobs this good aren't easy to come by."

He kissed her hair, her ear, her neck, and held her close. She would never forget.

"Dear God," he whispered. "The payment for sin is too heavy. Why, God? Why did You have to bring her to me so I could love her, and not be able to have her?"

She had never heard such words from him before. She never knew his feelings for her went so deep. She knew he loved her, but she didn't know her love could cause him such pain. His love and pain opened her eyes.

Abortion it would be. "We have no other options, I know. I love you, Ross."

His mouth pressed tightly on hers, hungering for the touch, the warmth, the love she could give. And she needed his.

A light sprinkle brought Joann reluctantly back to the present. "We'd better get back, Nicole. You aren't dressed for this." She tucked Nicole's blanket around her, and then wiped the tears from her own cheeks. "Dreams don't always have happy endings, Nicole. But we never stop hoping."

The stroller bumped back toward home.

·27·

··Four quiet days passed. Too quiet. Joann missed David's affection. She missed his conversation. He would come home from work, turn on the TV, pick up the newspaper, and ignore her. He didn't speak to Nicole either, but he held her and rocked her, whispering things into her ear when he didn't know Joann watched. On the fifth evening, David came home from work early.

He took Joann's hand, leading her to the couch. "Sit here. I'll make you some coffee."

Bewildered, Joann didn't know if she should question his early homecoming.

David brought her the coffee. "Tell me about the abortion."

Joann froze. She tried to block the feelings that pushed their way to the surface—the unresolved love for Ross, the impending fear of the abortion, guilt, and more fear.

David sat, looking at her with a blank face. She didn't know how to read it. Angry? Cold? Aloof? Kind?

"I want details this time."

Joann closed her eyes, then began.

"I remember it was bitter cold that day. As we were going into the clinic, Ross grabbed my hand and squeezed it. He was concerned and a bit afraid. We both shook. We knew if anyone found out, it would destroy both our futures. He tried to talk to me before we went in the building but couldn't. So much needed to be said, so much could not be said.

"The clinic people were nice, but they had a job to do. One woman even stood by my bed, holding my hand. She helped me keep in control of myself. I wanted to scream for the doctor to stop. I even whispered a faint, 'stop, please stop.' The doctor didn't stop. I don't think he even heard me.

"I could hear the machine drone. I felt like I was in a nightmare. The pain was strong, but not unbearable. Inside though, I felt hate swelling up. I hated myself more than I ever dreamed possible. And as the hate grew, something else died. A part of me went flat. Dead. Gone. Not just the baby, but a part of *me*. I wanted to roll over, curl up in a ball, but the doctor wasn't quite done."

Joann cried, her grief spilling over, deep and black. David stroked her hair, tears rolling down his face. With his other arm, he held Nicole. Joann sniffed, then went on.

"I sat on the edge of the table, trying to be strong, like they wanted me to be. They were all smiles now. The dirty part was over, let's smile. The evil is in a jar, let's smile. Oh, David, how I hated myself. I hated myself more for the relief I felt. How could I feel relieved when this child was gone? But relief filled me, swept over me, consumed me. It did everything relief is supposed to do, except make me feel better about myself. I forced myself to think about Ross, his love for me, and the desperation that drove us to that place.

"In the recovery room, a tiny woman brought me punch and a package of cookies. She took my blood pressure, pulled a blanket over me, and went to the next bed, to the new arrival. Little cramps tugged at my insides. I hated the fresh memory with each tug. I cried. The little woman came back and asked me how I felt.

" 'Relieved,' I told her. My cheeks grew hot and I looked away, horrified at what I had just said.

" 'That's okay,' she said to me. 'Everyone feels relief. That's not wrong. It's normal.'

"She must have noticed me double over a bit with one of the cramps and offered me a pain pill.

"I took it. I didn't need it for the pain, but I needed it to numb the rest of me.

"As I swallowed the pill with the punch, I decided. I would never let this get me down. I did the best I could. I considered all the choices, but there were none. No one would ever know, or need to know.

"After that, I stopped going to class. It hurt too much to see Ross in front, trying to act like nothing in life had changed, that teaching psych was the most consuming thing in his life. I could only think of what we had done. We were successful. No one was hurt. No secrets were discovered. But our futures *were* changed. Our strong love was killed in a few brief minutes in a clinic twenty miles away.

"So," she said, turning to David, "do you forgive me?"

"It will take time, Joann. I can't find out that I was not the only man you ever slept with, that you've killed a child, and forgive and forget overnight. Yes, I want to forgive you, yes, I will forgive you. But it will take time. And forget? I don't know if I can. Have you ever forgotten?"

"No. My nightmares remind me. Nicole reminds me. Los Angeles reminds me. And, oh God, how Carolyn reminds me."

"Your nightmares. They're from the abortion?"

"Yes, I dream of the abortion sometimes, and sometimes I see a baby waving at me."

David shook his head in disbelief. "And you were going to help Vicki suffer the same as you have?"

Protesting sobs poured out. "I thought I made the best decision in spite of the cost. While sitting at the clinic, I decided I might be wrong."

"Have you asked God to forgive you?"

"I asked for His help back then. I felt it was His guidance that led me to the clinic."

"God doesn't lead anyone to sin, Joann."

"It was the only choice I had."

David threw his arms up in the air. "Forget it, Joann. You have justified it to yourself so many times, there is no way you can admit what really happened. Until you can admit you were wrong, I think you'll continue to hurt the way you do."

"Nothing will ever take away that pain."

"Maybe not. But you need to forgive yourself. Excusing yourself and forgiving yourself are two different things. You excuse and minimize what you don't want to admit is wrong. You forgive yourself when you admit that what you did is wrong, but that it has no bearing on who you are today."

"Oh, but it *does* have a bearing on who I am. If I truly did something horrible back then, then I don't deserve to live, to claim to be a Christian, or be a 'good' person."

"Joann . . ."

The phone rang, freeing her to bury her feelings and escape the stuff David said that sounded like truth. Truth unfaceable.

·28·

AFDC, WIC, Medi-cal, foreign language a month ago, now a lifesaver for Vicki. "You know," Joann said to David, "this help is giving Vicki the strength she needed to see she can make it through the pregnancy. She'll make her decisions about what to do with the baby later. I'm so proud of her."

"So am I. It can't be an easy decision, no matter what her choice."

"David, it concerns me that the thing she needs most is lacking."

"What's that, babe?"

"Counseling. Someone to tell her all the ramifications of each choice, someone to take her through the system—that jungle of paper work. She needs to know all her options, and there's no one to help her."

"And she isn't the only one. Think of all the other teens who are in the same position. No wonder abortion is so appealing. Faced with the obstacles of carrying the baby, giving birth, then caring for it, or adoption, it's easier to give up. When is she going to tell her parents?"

"I'm going over there this afternoon. I'm scared."

"I'll be praying for you . . . and Vicki."

"Thanks."

"Is the bed all set up for her, just in case?"

"When Teresa and Dan found out yesterday, they begged Vicki to stay with them. She would have her own bedroom and bath there. It seemed like a better situation than our place."

David folded the newspaper. "I wish she'd stay here."

"Me too. But they're right. Here she'd have to share a room with Nicole, or Nicole would have to move into our bedroom again."

"At least she'll be close."

*　*　*

A grouchy, skinny version of Ma Kettle opened the door to greet Joann. Vicki's mother smiled through yellow cracked teeth when she saw the baby. "Well, Joann, ya brought the baby with ya. I've been askin' Vicki when ya'd bring her again. I've missed her. What's she been doin' new?"

The two women talked as they found a place to sit in the dusty, dark trailer. Joann hated bringing her sweet-smelling baby into this home. She emerged smelling like she'd been smoking in a hovel somewhere. "*Vicki*, ya got company," Mrs. Randolph yelled. She cooed and kissed Nicole while Joann winced. Nicole seemed to turn away when Mrs. Randolph's face came too close, blowing whiskey breath in her face. Mrs. Randolph patty-caked with the little hands, as Nicole cooed and gurgled back. After a few more minutes of weather and baby chat she hollered, "*Vicki. Ya comin'?*"

Vicki appeared, her wet hair pulled over her shoulders, as she drew her comb through it. "Hi, Joann," she tried to sound casual. "How long have you been here? I've been in the shower."

"Just a few minutes."

"Look at this baby, Vicki. Ain't she sweet? Babies are the sweetest things."

Vicki and Joann exchanged glances. Joann drew a deep breath. "Mrs. Randolph I've come to talk to you about something that's important."

"Ya want Vicki to baby-sit all night? I keep tellin' her as long as we don't tell Dad, then it'll be okay. Only because I know you, Joann."

"Thank you."

"Vicki, whatcha just standin' there for? Ya tryin' to be rude?"

"Mom, Joann's here to help me talk to you."

"Talk about what?"

"That I'm pregnant."

She looked up for the first time from the baby. "No ya ain't."

"She is, Mrs. Randolph. Twelve weeks along."

"I always knew you were nothin' but a little tramp, Vicki. Well, you ain't bringing no little brats home for me to take care of. You can just go get rid of it. We can't afford no baby." She stood up, carrying Nicole like damaged goods, dropping her into Joann's lap. She went to Vicki and got nose to nose. "You'll get an abortion now, won't ya?"

Vicki shook. "I'm not going to get an abortion, Mom."

Mrs. Randolph's voice shook the walls. "Oh, yes you are!"

Vicki's look pleaded with Joann for help. "Mom, I'm not."

Joann spoke. "Mrs. Randolph, I understand that you can't pay the doctor bills. I've been checking around. There are people who can help."

"She's *not* having a baby."

"She is, and we can't stop it."

"Sure we can, and we will."

"Mrs. Randolph, don't you think what Vicki wants is important?"

"If she's so selfish as to get pregnant, then she's not thinking about us, why should I think about her? She can just get out."

"Won't you reconsider?"

"There's no daughter of mine that gets pregnant. I told her that before. She gets pregnant, she's on her own. Now get!"

"I'm all packed."

Her mother looked surprised. "Packed?"

"Yes. I knew what your answer would be."

"Where will you go?"

"I didn't think you'd care." Vicki went to her room to get her things while Joann and Mrs. Randolph stood in awkward silence. Vicki kissed her surprised mother on the cheek as Joann opened the door. "Tell Dad I love him."

"I ain't tellin' him nothin'."

Emotion filled the silence in the car during the ride to Joann's. The rain splattered on the car, Vicki's tears splattered on her jacket. The outcome was no surprise, but the pain was.

·29·

week later, David bounced Nicole on his knee. "Oh, by the way," he said. "Carolyn called while you were gone. She wanted to meet you at the church around three. Something about the next Bible-study luncheon. You two are in charge of advertisement. She has a bunch of stuff she wants you to help put up on the bulletin board."

"Oh," Joann replied. "Did she say who the guest would be?"

"I didn't ask. I'm not doing anything this afternoon, so Nicole can stay with me."

Joann hesitated. She hated to leave Nicole—still. But as part of her plan to grow, and let go of Nicole, she had to. "Thanks," she said.

The overcast sky, holding an unshed spring storm, made the inside of the empty church dark and eerie. Joann hoped Carolyn would be on time. She felt silly with her childish fears of the dark and quiet, but couldn't shake them. She peeked around each corner, waiting for the boogeyman to jump out and scare her. Or maybe a real man intent on some evil. It was too quiet. The sound of her own breathing and walking echoed in the hall.

"Carolyn?" she called, not expecting an answer from her, but maybe from someone else.

Her steps became slower, more cautious. There was something to be afraid of, she knew. But what?

She rounded the last corner, and as she saw the bulletin board, a scream caught in her throat. A photograph of tiny body parts lying in a mangled heap was framed in yellow, like a party announcement. The cut-out letters of Psalms 139:13,15 NIV, stapled next to the photograph, screamed at her.

> FOR YOU CREATED MY INMOST BEING, YOU KNIT ME TO-GETHER IN MY MOTHER'S WOMB .... MY FRAME WAS NOT HIDDEN FROM YOU WHEN I WAS MADE IN THE SECRET PLACE.

The room reeled, the stench of blood filled Joann's nostrils. Blood and antiseptic. Her mind flung her back to the abortion clinic where her ears ached with the high-pitched sound of a machine turned on for a few, terrifying, painful seconds.

"Don't worry, it's almost over," she could again hear the nurse whisper. The tears rolled down her face and puddled in her ears. As the machine turned off, relief poured into her.

But now, guilt and anguish replaced the relief. "I killed my baby," she whispered out loud unknowingly. "No tissue, a baby. Oh God. Oh God."

She heard a sound behind her. It didn't register through the torment of emotion.

"God, I didn't know. What have I done?"

A funny, strangled noise startled Joann from behind. Her heart racing, she spun around, the tears in her eyes blurring and distorting the image of Carolyn. She sobbed, "Oh, Carolyn," her arms reaching to hug.

A strong, quick movement slapped Joann's arms away. "*You* had an *abortion?*" Carolyn screamed. "How could you? How could you lie, and deceive, and be so evil?"

"Carolyn," Joann tried to explain. "I didn't think I had any other choice."

"You knew. You knew exactly what you were doing. And to think I felt sorry for you when you had your miscarriage. You don't deserve to have any children. Much less an angel like Nicole."

"I know, I'm sorry."

"You aren't sorry, or you wouldn't have done it!"

"Carolyn, I really didn't know. It was horrible. So scary."

"Don't you realize what you put that baby through?"

"Shut up, Carolyn," Joann choked through her tears. "I can't change the past."

"You prissy little Christian hypocrite. So smug in your handwork doled out to everyone. A murderer."

Joann hung her head, feeling each word as a blow to her soul. She felt battered, bruised, and deserving of it all.

Carolyn's anger grew and fed upon itself instead of calming down. A contrite Joann dared lift her head. "Will you forgive me, Carolyn?"

"NEVER!" The sobs came from somewhere deep inside as Carolyn stormed out the door and down the church steps. Joann watched as the Camaro screeched through the parking lot. She slipped into a classroom and sunk to the floor, her sobs racking her body harder than she ever experienced before. "Oh God. Oh God," she cried. As the room grew dim, her body tired of grief. "Oh God, will You, can You forgive me? Oh God, I'm sorry. I'm so sorry. Oh God. I killed my baby. It was evil, there was no right anywhere.

"Oh God, forgive me for deceiving myself all these years, for denying the sin, the evil, the fact that I killed my child, Your child. I did have another choice, and I denied it. I denied the truth. I denied You. Oh God, forgive me."

Joann forced herself off the floor, feeling a strange peace and quiet wrap itself around her pain. She got home in a numb state. She went straight to Nicole, picking up the excited little girl, and sitting on the couch, rocking as if they were in the rocking chair. "David," she called, her voice no more than a whimper. "David. Come help me."

David emerged from the nursery, diaper, changing pad, and wipes in his hands. "What is it, babe?"

"Oh, David, I killed my baby. I killed my baby."

David held her, stroking her hair. He couldn't say, "It's okay," because it wasn't okay. But he could love her. "What happened?"

"At church. The bulletin board. The next Bible-study luncheon is going to have a movie. On abortion. It was so awful."

"What, babe?" he encouraged.

"There was a picture, of babies, after the abortion. I guess I've never really thought. I never. . . ."

"You never put your choice together with the result, did you?"

"No. But God help me, I have now. I killed my baby. A child as sweet as Nicole. I did it. How can I ever go on?"

"God loves you, Joann. He hasn't left you."

"But can He forgive me? I asked Him over and over, but can He ever? I've always thought of murderers as the lowest scum of the earth. And I am one, aren't I?"

"Joann, I love you. God loves you. Of course He's forgiven you."

"Maybe not. Carolyn won't."

"Of course she will. Why do you think she won't?"

"She saw me there, she told me she won't. She called me horrible things."

Joann explained the whole scene to David.

* * *

The day ended in slow, ugly reality. Her heart dragged in the dirt behind her as she walked. The door to her self-hate flung open, pouring accusations on her, all deserved, she thought. She opened her Bible, reading and rereading Psalms 139, punishing herself over and over.

She let David put Nicole to bed, and put herself to bed at eight o'clock, unable to face herself for one more minute. If she died in her sleep, it would be for the best. But she knew she would never get what she deserved. Only better.

When David came to bed, he wrapped his arms and legs around her, his tears rolling from his face into her hair. He cried for what she had done, he cried for the truth he hated, and he cried because the woman he loved hurt. And he didn't know how to help.

·30·

.. Carolyn could hardly see the road, her eyes dimmed with anger. "How could she?" she screamed at God. "My own best friend, a murderer. No wonder. No wonder she sided with them. I should have known."

She screeched around a corner, raced up the hill toward the freeway. "What a disgrace to Billy's name, to *Your* name, God."

She entered the freeway going north to Highway 85, then west to Morristown. She passed slow cars on the curves, nearly forcing a couple of them off the road. "How could she kill a baby? How could she do it?"

Her angry thoughts wove themselves together into hate. Her weapon of hate grew until it became a finely tuned weapon of warfare.

"My new tactic," she thought with a smile. "For Billy, for God, for me."

She whipped her car around in a dirt shoulder, then raced back toward home. She stopped at the stationery store to buy a piece of yellow poster board. "Thanks, Sally," she said to the cashier. "Isn't it amazing how just about everyone is giving in to worldly pressures these days?"

Sally looked up from the register. "What do you mean?"

Carolyn shrugged. "I guess I thought that Christians, at least, would stand for what is right."

"Well, don't they?"

Carolyn reached in her purse for the proper change. "I suppose if they don't, they don't let anyone know about it."

"Why that's sin! Deceit!"

"What do we do about it? One of our own church members is daily serving the community, making meals for new mothers, quilts for babies, handcrafts for just about everyone, as though she never had an abortion. As a church, should we tolerate such hypocrisy?"

Sally stood aghast. "Joann? Are you telling me Joann Simpson had an abortion?"

Carolyn dropped her eyes dramatically, her voice whispering, as if speaking to herself. "Oh, my, have I said too much?" Then in a normal tone, "The point is, how do we handle such disgrace in the church? Such deliberate trespassing of God's laws?" She stopped midsentence, and closed her purse. "I'm sorry, Sally. Such discussions are not for stationery-store lines. Please forgive me for my indiscretion."

On the way to her car, Carolyn smiled at the look of shock on Sally's face. It felt so good, she thought she'd make a few more stops on the way home.

She went to the deli to buy fresh imported cheese for a fondue dinner. As the owner waited on her, she gave him the same story she had given Sally. As an elder of the church, he seemed properly angered, Carolyn thought.

She found errands to do at the library, grocery store, and ice cream shop. At the church, she sat at the secretary's desk to use felt-tip pens to create a new poster. Then she mounted it next to the advertisement for the coming Bible study on abortion. She smiled, satisfied. "That ought to do it."

·31·

..Teresa came home from work to find her house clean, and Vicki setting the table. "Vicki. This wasn't part of the agreement."

"So who cares? I didn't have any homework. It won't kill me to help out a little bit."

"Thanks. How nice not to have to worry about that mess."

"I'll let you cook though. I'm not real good at that yet."

Teresa took off her shoes. "Don't worry about that. You've got lots of learning years ahead of you."

The phone rang.

Teresa sighed. "I don't need to talk to anyone, either. Will you get that for me, Vicki, and take a message?"

"Sure."

Teresa walked to her bedroom, pulling out the turquoise ribbon that held back her long hair. She unzipped her uniform top and pulled off the pants. She took a long, loose-fitting gauze dress from the closet, and pulled it over her head. She reached for her uniform to hang it up and stopped at the strain in Vicki's voice.

"No, I won't tell her that. I can't believe you'd say . . . no, I'm not. . ."

Teresa picked up the extension. "Hello?"

"Hi, Teresa," Carolyn's voice sang. "We've got a church problem to discuss."

"What kind of problem?"

"One of hypocrisy in the life of a person in our church who pretends to do good deeds for the church, in essence, feeding the poor, making quilts for babies, handcrafts for just about everyone—"

Vicki broke in. "I told you not to say anything."

"—all the while hiding a past abortion. I think we should get together and discuss it further. Oh, I'll have to call you back another time. Rob just walked in the door, and we have an engagement to attend. Bye!"

Teresa's heart crumbled. She held the receiver to her ear, not paying attention to Vicki yelling at the dial tone. She saw instead the sadness in Joann's eyes, the tears, her avoiding Carolyn when she talked of abortion. She put the receiver down. She sat on the bed, her knees pulled up underneath her chin. Tears rolled down her face.

Vicki stamped into the room. "Some friend, telling Joann's secrets. I know what I'd like to do to that . . . that . . . I never liked her anyway. I always knew there was something strange about her, Miss High and Mighty Perfect Lady. I hope she rots, I really do. . . ."

Teresa heard Vicki's voice, but could only think of Joann. "I'm going over there, Vicki. If Dan comes home, tell him I'll be back in a minute."

She knocked several times on the door before David answered. He looked worn and tired.

"Can I see Joann, David?"

He looked blankly at her, then said quietly, "Just a minute."

He returned a moment later. "She said she doesn't want to see anybody."

"Tell her I love her, okay?"

David looked confused. "Why that?"

"Just tell her. I'll talk to you later, maybe tomorrow, okay?"

The next day, Teresa tried calling Joann several times, and knocked on her door with no response.

At work, her mind remembered the women whose abortions she had assisted—thinking of Joann as one of them. Their situations ran through her mind—mothers, threatened with desertion if they had one more child, women over forty, afraid of the outcome, and the scores of teenagers and young women, in desperate situations—frightened and confused. Where did Joann fit in?

She tried to be friendly with the dental patients, but found herself not speaking to them.

A gossipy woman from church was their last patient. She worked at the stationery store. "Sally," Teresa said politely. "How are you today?"

"Oh, not well. I have this tooth back here that aches when I eat. I'm sure it will have to come out."

Teresa restrained her remarks. "I'll take an X ray for the doctor. We'll see if there's a cavity."

As she set up the machine, and stuck the plastic square in Sally's mouth, Sally's eyes suddenly lit up. She pointed at the film.

"I'll take it out in a moment. We only have one to take. You can tell me in a minute." She took the picture, then pulled the film from Sally's mouth. "What did you need to say, Sally?"

"Well," she exclaimed in her righteous voice. "Did you know that Joann Simpson had an abortion? I'm telling you, you never can tell these days. Here she is, acting so pious, cooking meals, always do-gooding when she has done this terrible thing."

Teresa staggered back. "Who told you?"

Sally smiled, "A very reliable source—her best friend, Carolyn."

Teresa closed her eyes, her shoulders drooping.

"And," chirped Sally, "I was at church last night and noticed a poster on the bulletin board. It said, 'Joann Simpson to share her abortion experience after the movie.' I bet there'll be a real crowd there!"

"I'd better go develop this," Teresa said. She ran to the darkroom, and put the film in the developing machine. "Oh, God, what has happened to Carolyn? And Sally, Lord. If this wasn't a professional place, I'd tell her off, then punch her. She's so *happy* about this. Happily disgusted."

It took the doctor a few minutes to fill the tiny cavity. Teresa was glad the drill wasn't her responsibility.

She finished her work for the day and drove to the church to remove the poster from the bulletin board. She ripped it up, throwing it in an outdoor trash can. Then she went to see David at the market.

"Can we talk in the back?" she asked him.

"Is it important?"

Teresa nodded.

"Okay. We're not supposed to take anyone back there, but I've got some work I can do. Maybe they won't complain."

David set himself up to trim lettuce. "What's up?" he asked.

"I know about Joann's abortion."

The knife stopped. "Did she tell you?"

"No, Carolyn did."

David jammed the knife into a head of lettuce. "No!" he whispered.

"And, David, I thought you should know since Joann will know soon enough."

"What else?"

"Carolyn has told lots of people . . . strategic people."

"Like who?"

"Sally."

"No," he said again.

Tears came to her eyes. "She also put up a poster at church, promising Joann would be the guest speaker at the luncheon . . . to share her abortion experience. I've taken it down, but who knows how many people have already seen it."

"Why would she do that to Joann?"

"Carolyn has been so angry since Billy died. My guess is she wants to get back at the world for abortion. Now she can vent her anger on a specific person. I'm so sorry Joann is her target."

David nodded. "You might be right. Carolyn told Joann she'd never forgive her."

Teresa shook her head. "That's what she needs the most—forgiveness."

·32·

··Joann held her teddy bear while Nicole slept. She stared out the window, through the oak trees at the lake. The empty lot looked beautiful with the green weeds and wild flowers growing all over it. She watched the breeze blow gently over the tops, stroking them in wide bands.

"I'll never go out again. How can I?" she said to Teddy. "Last night was the final blow. Everyone knows. A poster at church. My best friend betrayed me."

She put Teddy on the bed when Nicole woke. She looked at her baby, Nicole's whole body smiling at her mother, and said, "You have a bad person for a mother, Nicole. I don't deserve to have you. I've done a horrible thing."

She felt like crying, but her tears had dried up. When David tried to hug her as she sat on the couch, she'd curl up in a little ball. Afraid to be touched, afraid to be rejected.

Each day she thought over her abortion again and again. She thought of the options she had had, and how she refused to choose. She looked at it from every angle to see what she had done, what she had needed and didn't receive. She thought about Vicki and shivered, thinking of how close she came to helping Vicki choose years of pain.

She went to her room, taking a small notebook from her dresser drawer, and began to write. Her writing over the next few days proved to be a kind of therapy.

April 12th. I don't know what else to do but write my feelings down somewhere. I can't talk to anybody even though everyone knows my secret, thanks to Carolyn.

It's funny how all the feelings I had way back then are not gone. I only stuffed them away. They've oozed their way out in the most peculiar ways and at the strangest times. They are so out of place.

April 14th. I hate it. I hate thinking about it. My stomach tightens. I don't want to think about what happened then. I want to pretend this isn't happening to me now. But it is. What am I supposed to do about it? I want to hide. The problem is too big for me.

April 15th. Tax day. The day to pay up what you owe. How can I ever pay what I owe?"

April 18th. Dear Carolyn, Have you ever done something you thought was right, but it turned out to be wrong—terribly wrong? I suppose not.

My heart is sick. My insides writhe and groan. How could I have been so blind? So stupid? To change the past is impossible. Can I change the future to alleviate the past? I don't know if it's possible.

Was I daydreaming back then? Rationalizing? I hate myself. I hate my stupidity, I hate those blinders I put on. . . .

April 19th. I take the memory with me everywhere . . . my invisible scarlet letter A. Scarlet for my baby's blood, A for abortion.

April 21st. Melancholy wins today. I can't seem to chase the mood away. It hangs not over, but inside me. Not weighing me down particularly, just there and dark. It's hard to smile, hard to see anything positive about the future.

The mood feels permanent. I don't think I can scrape up the energy to accomplish anything anyway.

Choices. I hate them. I hate to fail. Listen to me complain. Like I said, melancholy wins.

* * *

Joann heard David open the front door. She closed the book she was reading and stretched before getting off the bed. She tried to be pleasant to him, as the only person she could trust. These last three weeks, she knew he had forgiven her. She could feel his sadness, but he held her tighter than before. He listened to her, and she listened to him. She started to share his dreams again, because she could have none of her own.

She pulled her slippers on and scuffed out to the living room. Seated on the couch were Teresa and two women she had never seen before. She whirled around to disappear into the bedroom once more. David caught her arm. "I want you to talk to Teresa."

"No."

"She brought some people who can—"

"No."

Teresa jumped off the couch and ran to Joann. She threw her arms around her and squeezed. "I love you, Joann. I love who you are today. What is in the past is gone. God has forgiven you. So has David and so do I."

Joann began to shake. "You can't forgive me, it's too horrible to forgive."

"I *can* forgive you. I had to forgive myself. Come over here and sit down."

Joann slumped in David's chair. Teresa sat cross-legged on the floor in front of her. "I used to work in an abortion clinic."

Joann lifted her head to look at Teresa, amazed at what she heard.

"I can't believe how stupid, how naive I was. I heard they scraped out tissue, and that was it. I didn't know the baby was alive, with a heartbeat and moving. I wanted so much to help. I listened to the hurting women, to help them in their struggles.

"For many years I couldn't forgive myself for what I had done. It's still a battle sometimes, and always will be. I hated myself for so long. Dan helped me to see that when I realized the God of the universe forgave me, then what right did I have to condemn myself? I had to see that the bad thing I did back then is not connected to what I do now. I am not continuing to do that wrong. I am admitting that wrong, and searching to do what is right. I haven't found my niche yet, but I will."

Joann looked at the two women who wore soft expressions of concern. "Who are they?" Joann asked Teresa.

"They are two women I have met in my search for what to do in my battle against abortion. Jennifer is a member of WEBA, Women Exploited by Abortion. It's an organization of over twenty thousand women who are helping each other through the emotional pain of their decision to abort. I thought you might want to join the local group. It's a sort of self-help group. She is also a pro-life worker."

Joann flinched, her head pulled back.

"And this is Marilyn. She, too, is a pro-life worker."

Joann set herself up for attack. Marilyn spoke. "We wanted to come give our support to you. Jennifer has had an abortion, but I haven't. We feel the same about abortion. I want you to know we care. I also want to ask you not to judge all our workers by one. We all have our different approaches and ways of doing things. I know one of our members has hurt you, and I am sorry. It is not our policy to act in such a manner toward those who have been deceived by the abortionists."

A weight seemed to disappear from inside Joann's spirit. She turned to Teresa. "What about everyone else in this town? I've lost my credibility and Christian witness. No one wants to be around me anymore."

Teresa nodded. "Sure, there are a few who feel that way. But I think you'll be surprised at how many tears have been shed on your behalf. So many people have approached me, asking how they can contact you. They want to give you their support. So many want you to tell about your experience. They feel they can learn how to help others from you."

Joann drew up her knees. "Oh, I couldn't do that."

"Not yet. Maybe never. But I think you'll find healing and acceptance by telling why you made your choice. I think you'll be able to help others, as Jennifer does, in showing how you can forgive yourself and go on with life."

God's peace filled Joann as she allowed herself to be forgiven. She got up to pull the drapes open. "It's too dark in here. I'm going to let some light in."

She hugged Teresa and went to make a pot of coffee for her guests.

* * *

April 23. Teresa came over with some friends today. There is a future; there is a hope! God has forgiven me. Now, can I forgive myself?

April 25. I couldn't go to sleep last night. I was so upset. I went out on the deck and cried and sobbed and prayed. God opened my ears to hear Him. "I am forgiven," whispered out in puffs into the cold night air. "Forgetting what lies behind, reaching forward to what lies ahead." He loves me, so today I am at peace. Not deliriously happy—just satisfied that I am in God's care.

My life will never be the same. But I am forgiven.

Epilogue

"This is a lot different from our first anniversary celebration, isn't it?" David asked with a smile.

"Or the second," Joann replied. "This is everything I ever hoped an anniversary would be."

"How's that?"

Joann snuggled next to him. "Romantic. Linen tablecloth, candles, flowers, privacy, and lots of love."

"I'm for all those things. Especially the last. I like this train car. When did you say you ate here before?"

"My birthday, last year."

David nodded, then took a drink from his water glass. "This has been an interesting year. I think we could be celebrating more than an anniversary."

Joann dipped her fork into her salad. "Year one we celebrated moving. Year two . . ." Joann blushed and looked down.

"We didn't celebrate at all," David answered for her. "We should have celebrated honesty, because that gave us cause to celebrate year three."

Joann kissed his cheek. "Thanks for all your forgiveness. I can't believe it was easy to forgive the abortion, the deceit, the damage to our relationship." Joann rolled her eyes. "And my obsessions . . . blocking you out of my life. How could you stand me?"

"It wasn't easy, but it was worth it."

Joann punched him softly on his arm. "Really, David, you've taught me how precious forgiveness is. Not everyone can forgive."

"Are you still troubled about Carolyn?"

"I think I'm still grieving. It's hard to be so close, and then have the relationship end suddenly."

"An unfinished symphony." *The only unfinished symphony left in my life.*

"You know," David told her. "You and Teresa have done a terrific job pulling that Crisis Pregnancy Center together."

"We couldn't have done it without the church's support, and that of some kind citizens in town. And all the donations that flood in! Today we got two cribs, six boxes of baby clothes, and three high chairs. I'm amazed at the generosity."

"I'm amazed at you—how you've taken an ugly experience and are using it to help others."

"It's a good feeling, helping these women. We've chosen to help both the woman and the unborn baby, not focus all our energies on one or the other. Teresa is so excited about doing something positive to turn the abortion statistics around. And the women! After they tough through the first three months, they are so happy they have chosen life—even those who plan adoption."

"And how's Vicki? I haven't seen her in a couple of weeks. Did she get the job at the dress shop?"

"Yes! I saw her today when she came in to volunteer at the center. She starts work on Monday. I hope this job works out better than the last one."

"Her little girl is so cute."

Joann's eyes filled with tears. "Yes she is. And to think . . ."

"We've got a lot to be thankful for." David held Joann's hand. "I know I'm thankful to have a wife. A healthy wife."

Confused, Joann protested. "I've always been healthy."

David's face grew stern. "Your heart was sick. It almost destroyed the best part of you."

"I *was* awfully sick inside. It took a long time to get me moving toward healing, though. Too long." She shook her head. "I didn't realize what kind of gem I married. I was stupid in more ways than one."

They both worked on their salads for a few bites. A thought came to Joann. "Oh, David. I forgot to tell you, I haven't had a nightmare in eight months!" *And I haven't thought about Ross in seven, and that was to say good-bye.*

David wiped his mouth. "I've noticed. Things are changing, Joann. We're growing."

"Yeah," Joann said. *I'm finally leaving it all behind.*